The Borrowed God

&

Other Stories

(Revised Edition)

JYOTI PRATEEK

Contents

Foreword

I was soared and taken away into lands of mysticism and wisdom, where elements were speaking to my soul. Miraculous landscapes, unassuming saints and ancient temples were filling my mind with long forgotten wisdom. I felt as if enlightened Masters talked to me as I was a child and they were my parents.

"Is it possible that all these words were written by a modest and humble lady from a different side of the world?" I questioned myself. How old this soul must be when she pours such a great wisdom with so much grace and humility?

I surrendered to her voice and words and allowed myself to be taken into heights and depths of eternal Truth. Blessed is the being that spread so much light unto this world. Blessed are all those who have the chance to be illuminated by it.

Keep shining, you beautiful Soul, whoever touches your words and stories, will be changed forever.

- Milan Bojic,
Editor in chief, The Awakening Times magazine

Preface

From the feet of my Guru to the cave of my thoughts, from the pages of my personal diary to Facebook notes, and finally to The Awakening Times, the words of these stories have come a long way. They stem from ancient, timeless wisdom, channelled through my personal reflections and woven into stories for a relatable experience.

The Indian scriptures abound in stories that personify elements, virtues, and vices in simple narratives to illuminate the profound truths of life for all. While interviewing Sri Vedayana for The Awakening Times about his treatise on the Rig Veda, I was inspired by how our ancients personified the basic elements of Nature and recognized the Universe as one Universal Being. This perspective beautifully brings out the concept of Oneness. While science deals with these elements objectively, viewing them as sentient beings makes them more alive and relatable.

In some of these stories, I have explored this style of personification, allowing the elements to come alive and share their own stories and perspectives. Some emerged from direct experience, others from imagination, and many are replete with symbolism and metaphors. Each story carries a message; a precious insight from the Universe, that impelled me to share it with everyone.

As I meditated, these stories kept evolving, unfolding new layers of understanding—at times leading me to rewrite them with the fresh perspectives they revealed. Even in print, they remain fluid, ever open to new interpretations.

This book is an offering to seekers on the path of awakening — inviting them to introspect, deepen awareness, instill values, and contemplate on the cycle of life and death. The stories here are only glimpses of the ever-unfolding lessons of Life. It is an invitation to the classroom of the Universe, where we continue to evolve beyond time and the need to graduate.

I extend my heartfelt gratitude to The Awakening Times and Milan, its Editor-in-Chief, for the platform and encouragement that helped shape this work.

My deepest thanks to Prateek, my co-traveler in this journey of lifelong learning. His honest critique, sincere support, and valuable insights have been immensely helpful.

With deep reverence to my Guru, Dr. S.R. Thakur, whose wisdom echoes through these pages, I dedicate this work to his vision of awakened and liberated souls.

Jyoti Prateek

God

Devotion

The Shiva temple on the banks of the river near the old Peepal tree was thronged by devotees morning and evening. The reflection of the morning sun colored the river waters orange, transforming it into an ascetic draped in flowing ochre robes, bowing in reverence to the temple of Shiva on its edge. Birds chirped on the tree as if chanting sacred hymns, while devotees from far and near arrived with offerings of flowers, fruits, milk and sweets to have a glimpse of their beloved deity.

The fragrance of incense sticks wafted through the air, mingling with the sound of temple bells. Bushes of Tulsi graced the entrance of the brick-floored shrine and at the center, stood the black, rock-solid *Shivalinga*. Water poured continuously onto it through a pierced copper vessel, keeping it perpetually bathed and clean. Devotees offered flowers and milk to the deity, bowing deeply in reverence, while ants feasted on bits of sweets left from the *prasad.*

Behind the main *mandap* of the temple, along the North wall, stood three banana trees in a neat row. At the end of this row was the simple and humble abode of Deenanath, the temple priest. Deenanath would wake up early each morning and after cleaning the temple and having his bath, he would sit for hours, chanting the name of his lord Shiva. His wife, Janaki, often accompanied him, and occasionally their son, Surya, would join them—though he rarely stayed awake for long and would soon drift back to sleep.

Deenanath and Janaki washed the temple daily and adorned it with fresh flowers which they grew in their small yard. Janaki prepared a sweet offering – the *prasad*, for the devotees, a ritual that kept the family happily busy. Surya, however, showed little interest in these practices. And Deenanath never imposed them on him. He believed that devotion was a bond to be developed like friendship, it could not be forced. To him, devotion was a spontaneous innate flowering that took its own time to grow and blossom.

As the years passed by, Deenanath grew anxious about the future of the temple. He knew his strength was waning and someone would need to take over his responsibilities to ensure the temple remained a place of solace for the devotees. He thought of Surya, who was now an independent young man, but he hesitated, knowing his son's lack of interest. Finally, one day, he broached the subject.

"Surya," he said gently, "I've been thinking about the temple. I'm growing older, and soon someone will need to take care of it. Would you consider stepping in?"

Surya frowned. "Baba, I don't think I can do this job."

"Why not, my son? What's wrong with it? You'll take up a job somewhere, won't you? This is no different, and you already know so much about it."

"It is different," Surya replied, in a voice tinged with frustration. "I know you've dedicated your life to this temple, but what has it given you in return? You work tirelessly from morning to evening, yet your efforts go unnoticed. The devotees bow to a rock statue, completely ignoring the man who makes this place what it is. I feel ashamed that our family lives on offerings made to a stone idol. Baba, it pains me to say this, but your status is less than that of a rock."

Deenanath was taken aback by his son's words. Though he was calm on the outside, he felt shattered inside. He took a deep breath and steadied himself before replying, "Surya, you are free to choose the work that brings you peace, but there is a misunderstanding I must address. I am not here for status or recognition. If I sought those, I would have never devoted my life to this temple. I am here because of my love for Lord Shiva, who has been my constant companion through life."

Though filled with emotions, Deenanath continued in a steady voice, "The devotees who come to this temple bring something far more precious than what you see. They bring with them the gift of devotion. Their eyes can see God in a rock, and that is not a small thing. *Bowing to something powerful is natural, but bowing to something considered ordinary or lifeless—like a rock—is an act of profound devotion.* Their faith feeds the devotee in me, and their offerings are not just material; they are tokens of love and reverence."

Deenanath's eyes moistened as he spoke, "Their devotion is what endears them to me. For me, being devoted is not a duty; it is my joy, my way of expressing love. I am happy to have a lifetime or more of devotion, as the creation of devotion is something as precious as God. Still, if you think that your status lies elsewhere, you are free to pursue your choice. Devotion cannot be forced, it is an inner flowering my son, if you don't feel it within, it means you aren't ripe for it yet. But I know the seed is within you and will wait for the right time."

Deenanath's words touched Surya's heart deeply. Tears welled in his eyes as he hugged his father tightly. "Baba, forgive me. I never saw things from your perspective. Devotion is indeed a subtle but strong thread that binds the Lord and the devotee. I now see the peace and strength it has given you. I too want to hold onto this thread. Please guide me so I can walk this path of devotion."

Father and son lit a lamp together in the temple that evening. The light of the lamp seemed to dispel not just the darkness of the shrine but also the doubts that had lingered in Surya's heart. That evening was no longer dark!

The Borrowed God

We borrow gods from outside
To realise the One within
When the One within is realised
The true worship begins

On the banks of river Sarayu, in the small village of Chitrakoot, lived a farmer named Dhaniram. He worked hard in the fields to meet the needs of his family and of those who came to him for help. Over the years he had experienced many ups and downs of farming—diseases that ravaged crops, hailstorms that destroyed the harvest, and sometimes when he was lucky, the joy of bountiful yields. Despite his experience and skill, worry was a constant companion in his life.

One day, on his way home, Dhaniram passed the village temple and noticed the priest, Nakulananda, humming a bhajan and moving about with an air of carefree joy. The sight stopped him in his tracks as he wondered how someone could live with such ease while his own days were weighed down by toil and anxiety. He stepped closer and asked, "Hey Nakula, how do you manage to be so joyous and carefree? I have never known such a state; I am either working hard in the fields or worried about my crops. Please share your secret so I may also benefit."

The priest smiled warmly and said, "It is no secret. I simply worship my God and leave the rest to Him. He takes care of everything."

Dhaniram's eyes widened in amazement. "You are so lucky! If you don't mind, can I borrow your God for a few days? Perhaps He can help me too."

Nakulananda was taken aback by this strange request. No one had ever asked him such a thing, and he didn't know how to respond. None of the scriptures he had studied offered instructions on how to loan a God! "This is such an odd question, how am I supposed to answer it? Moreover, what would a temple be without an idol if I give it to him?" The joy on Nakulananda's face was soon replaced by worry, as these thoughts flooded his mind.

After a moment of hesitation, he replied, "You cannot take the God of this temple. But, to keep you happy, I will give you a new God."

Nakulananda went inside the temple and picked up a stone he used as a paperweight. Handing it to Dhaniram, he said, "Here is your God. It's all between you and Him now."

Nakulananda was unsure about the results of giving this 'God' to Dhaniram so he added, "Remember, though, you must worship Him properly for Him to take care of you."

Overjoyed at the prospect of receiving God, Dhaniram said, "Thank you! Don't worry; I will worship Him with all my heart."

As Dhaniram happily walked home with the 'borrowed God' in his hands, he passed an old man sitting under a banyan tree. The man called out weakly, "Son, I haven't eaten anything since three days. God will bless you if you can feed some food to this hungry soul." Dhaniram glanced at him, but hurried homeward cradling the stone and constantly looking at it with admiration. His mind was too preoccupied with thoughts of carrying 'God' home and worshipping Him, that he ignored the earnest plea of the old man.

As he reached home, Dhaniram, excited to share the news, called out to his wife, "Look, I have brought God home! Now all our worries will disappear."

His wife was puzzled and asked "Where is He?" Dhaniram proudly held out the stone that the priest had given him. She looked at it and suppressed a smile. She understood that the priest had fooled her naïve husband. But she also knew that her husband's faith was pure and didn't want to discourage him. So she warmly said "That's wonderful."

Dhaniram asked her to bring food for God, saying he wouldn't eat until God had eaten. He bathed the stone and lovingly placed it on a small altar he had set up. He was delighted at the idea that God would eat food from his hands. Dhaniram was so simple; he never thought that a stone could not eat. In fact he never believed he brought home a stone, all he knew was, that he brought God home. He lovingly offered food to the stone. But the stone remained still, showing no sign of acceptance.

Disappointed, Dhaniram thought, "Perhaps I need to pray harder." Bowing deeply, he pleaded the stone to accept his offering, but nothing happened. "Maybe God likes bhajans," he thought, recalling Nakulananda's singing. And for the first time in his life, Dhaniram sang, but even his heartfelt effort seemed to leave God unimpressed. Shrouded in self-doubt, he assumed that his voice was coarse and not melodious enough to please God. So he decided to get a music system instead, to play bhajans. But even this did not seem to work, as the stone didn't move an inch to accept the offerings.

"Maybe God is uncomfortable in this humble hut," he thought. "I should arrange a better seating arrangement to please Him." Dhaniram went out to get some fine cloth and decorations to prepare a seat suitable for God. He spent the whole day preparing the altar. After that Dhaniram was so tired that he didn't know when he fell asleep. He went without food that day.

The next morning he woke up and saw that God had not tasted even a morsel of the food he offered. Determined to please God, he bathed the stone and dressed it in the new clothes he had brought. Placing the well clothed stone on the new altar, he offered it incense, flowers and fruits with soft bhajans playing on the music system. Dhaniram kept pleading God to accept his offerings, but the stone seemed insensitive to his cries. Three days passed by like this. Dhaniram too went without food. His wife grew worried and tried to persuade him to eat, but he refused, saying, "I cannot eat until God accepts my offering."

On the third day, the same old beggar arrived at their door, begging for food. Dhaniram's wife explained the situation to him, and said, "I'd feed you, but my husband hasn't eaten for days. How can I serve you when he himself is starving?"

The beggar looked at her with concern and said, "Take me to him."

Inside, they found Dhaniram kneeling before the altar, tears streaming down his face as he begged the stone to accept his devotion. Then suddenly, the old man walked up and kicked the stone aside, and sat on the altar himself.

Dhaniram stared in disbelief. For a moment, anger flared within him, but as he looked into the beggar's weary eyes, something shifted. He recalled the old man's plea for food and looked deeply at his own longing to serve God. Suddenly, it dawned on him: "The hunger I had ignored under the banyan tree is the same hunger I was trying to appease at home'.

In this flash of understanding, Dhaniram picked up the food meant for God and lovingly offered it to the old man. Tears of joy filled his eyes as the beggar ate. Afterwards, the beggar smiled, fed Dhaniram the remaining food, and said, "Now that you've fed me, shall we go to the fields?"

Dhaniram felt a sense of inexplicable peace. As they walked to the fields, he reflected on the events of the past few days. He realized that the stone had only been a medium to invoke God. The God he sought was not in the stone that he was trying to propitiate. The real God was within him and needed no appeasement. He was there to be experienced in the act of love and giving.

Later when he returned, his wife asked him "That beggar kicked your idol, yet you fed him? Why?"

Dhaniram smiled. "For a moment, I was angry. But then I understood —God wasn't in the stone or even in the temple. He was in my heart all along. It was the feeling of devotion within me that made me see God in both the stone and the man. If this devotion; this strong desire to serve Him, wasn't there, I wouldn't have seen God in either of them. So God isn't outside, He's always within us, waiting to be expressed through love."

The next day, Dhaniram walked to the temple to return the borrowed God. As he handed the stone back, Nakulananda asked, surprised, 'You're returning God so soon? Did He fail you?' Dhaniram shook his head and smiled. "No, Nakula. He succeeded. This borrowed God made me realize that the one I was seeking was always within me."

Nakulananda stood silent, humbled by the farmer's simple yet profound wisdom.

The Idol Maker

In the quiet village of Vishnupur, nestled between lush green fields and rolling hills, lived Rama, an idol maker whose creations seemed to breathe with divine life. For decades, Rama had sculpted idols for the temples in his village and neighbouring towns. Occasionally, city dwellers would come, marvel at his work, and purchase his idols to take back to their bustling lives. To Rama, idol-making wasn't just a livelihood—it was a passion. His hands moved with the precision of a master artist, and his heart poured life into stone. His idols seemed so alive that they could almost walk, speak, or bless those who stood before them. The magic of his handwork often left onlookers awestruck, compelled to bow in reverence.

Rama's devotion to his work was unmatched. He would often lose track of time, skipping meals and ignoring discomfort, fully absorbed in his art. Neither the summer heat or winter chill, nor hunger or fatigue could weaken his unwavering dedication. His wife often worried about his health, but she knew better than to disturb him when he was in his zone.

One afternoon, as Rama chipped away at a block of stone, shaping it into a new idol, his friend Bhola arrived. Bhola, a farmer, had known Rama since childhood and often stopped by to chat. Rama's wife brought out tea for the two friends, and Bhola watched as Rama's chisel danced over the stone.

Bhola, a devotee at heart, used to visit the village temple daily. He would religiously perform a *puja* ritual at sunrise before proceeding for work in the fields. He believed that if he missed out on the rituals, it would displease the gods, and the result of their displeasure would be a failed harvest or infected crop.

Bhola had always seen Rama engrossed in work and had never spotted him performing rituals to seek the favour of gods. He wondered how Rama's work went on smoothly without pleasing the gods and incurring any losses from their displeasure. Sheer curiosity made him ask, "Rama, you spend so much time creating these idols with devotion, but don't you ever take time to worship them?"

Rama paused, looking up from his work. "Worship them? Bhola, I create them, isn't this act of creation, a worship in itself? I pour my heart and soul into these idols. Isn't that devotion? People visit the temple for an hour to pray, but I spend days, even weeks, breathing life into these forms. If you define worship by rituals, then this—" he gestured toward the half-formed idol, "—is my ritual."

Bhola fell silent, pondering Rama's words. After a moment, he smiled and nodded. "You're right, my friend. We all have our ways of expressing devotion." He patted Rama on the back, finished his tea, and left for the fields.

The sun climbed higher and brighter, making the air warmer, as Rama finished the idol. He got up to stretch himself and saw the village schoolteacher, Masterji, coming his way. Masterji, known for his rational mind and skepticism toward idol worship, often visited Rama to admire his artistry.

On seeing him, Rama smiled to himself, knowing that Masterji's skeptical eyes would need a different lens to see the divine essence of his craft.

As Masterji neared Rama's house, Rama asked his wife to get some water, flowers, vermilion and incense sticks. Then Rama set aside his tools and began performing a *puja* ritual for worshipping the new idol.

Seeing Rama perform the ritual, Masterji took a seat near him and quietly waited for Rama to finish the ceremony.

"Namaste, Masterji," Rama greeted him, finishing the ritual.

Masterji greeted him with a smile. "Namaste, Rama. How are you today?"

"By God's grace, I am well. Please, accept this *prasad*." Rama said giving him the sweet offertory.

Masterji stepped closer, to accept the *prasad* while his eyes admired the beautiful idol Rama had just created. "Rama, you create beautifully! I am in awe of your craftsmanship. But I don't understand why you would need to perform a ritual to worship an idol that you created with your own hands? Isn't the process of creating it, an act of worship in itself? How can you expect a lifeless stone to bless you when it's your skill that brings it to life?"

Rama smiled. "Masterji, you're wise to ask that question. But tell me, if I, the creator, don't revere these idols, how can I expect others to? The purpose of making an idol is lost if I don't honour it myself. The ritual isn't just a customary act; it's my expression of respect for what the idol represents."

Rama's words made Masterji pause and think for a while. He realized that a ritual of reverence, even for one's own creation, could hold a deeper significance than he had considered.

He nodded slowly, impressed by Rama's perspective. "You have a point, Rama. You truly are an artist with wisdom." He stayed for a while, chatting about village matters, before heading back to school for the evening classes.

After Masterji left, Rama's wife, Sheela, who was silently witnessing the entire conversation approached him, "Dear, I didn't quite understand this. When Bhola asked why you don't perform a ritual like he does, you mentioned that creating the idol is the ritual in itself. While to Masterji, who was already in agreement to the fact that the process of creation is the ritual, you emphasized the importance of the ritual. Why?"

At this Rama laughed then explained, "Dear, both are true. Bhola and Masterji saw different parts of the picture. Bhola's faith needed to be complemented with the truth that work is worship. And Masterji's skepticism needed to see that reverence gives meaning to creation. I simply gave them the missing pieces to complete their understanding."

Sheela smiled, but had more to ask, "Your words make me wonder, dear. What truly drives you to create these idols? Is it devotion, livelihood, or something deeper?"

Rama's expression softened and he spoke with quiet conviction. "The truth, my love, is that all creation is born from bliss. I create these idols because it fills me with joy. The happiness of seeing your creation come to life is something unparalleled. It satiates the soul like nothing else. Worship and money are blessings that flow from that joy, but they are not my purpose. Bliss is the seed, and creation is its fruit. And in creating, I connect with the Divine who breathes life into the lifeless."

Sheela watched with quiet admiration as he returned to his work, the rhythmic tap of his chisel weaving a melody of devotion and bliss.

The Priest and the Cobbler

In a small town in northern India, lived a simple and contented man, named Ravidas. He repaired shoes in a small, thatched corner of the town market lane. A good night's sleep was his only treasure. He was happy with his life and had modest aspirations. All he desired were a few broken slippers or unpolished shoes each day, enough to earn him a belly-full meal.

He didn't have many friends, as he seldom visited the temple or joined the cobblers' *choupal* to chat or gamble. Instead, he believed that his hands, feet, and eyes were his best companions, and that was enough for him.

He went to bed as soon as the sky turned dark and woke only when the sun appeared on the horizon. So he had no need of any lamps, electric or otherwise. The sun and the moon were the only lamps that illuminated his humble abode. His food was wholly natural, comprising of fruits alone. So he didn't need to cook or clean the dishes. Such a simple and peaceful life made him feel like an emperor in his own right. Free-spirited Ravidas actually lived like one, though without a crown. He rolled in the luxuries of abundant quality time with himself, peace and good health.

It was festive season and the whole town was bustling with celebration. Deepavali was around the corner and lamps lit up every street. Firecrackers burst with sounds of joy, and homes gleamed with freshly painted walls, cleaned floors, and shimmering decorations. Yet, Ravidas' house remained unlit. He slept early, as always, and even the noise of the firecrackers couldn't rob him of his precious sleep.

Early next morning he went to the river for his bath. On his way, he noticed the streets strewn with the remnants of the celebrations: ashes from firecrackers, discarded sweet wrappers, wilted prayer flowers, and burnt-out lamps. He pondered at the futility of such celebrations which began with cleansing homes and streets and ended by creating such a mess that needed to be cleaned again. The sweepers were still asleep, exhausted from the night's festivities. Ravidas shrugged, took his bath, and returned home.

Knowing that no one would come to the town market early that day, he picked up a book and started reading. Ravidas loved reading scriptures and playing melodious tunes on his flute during his leisure hours.

As the sun rose higher, he made his way to his work corner in the marketplace. Most people from the town had visited the temple, the previous day, to make offerings and seek blessings of the Divine.

"Namaste, Panditji," Ravidas greeted the temple priest warmly as they crossed paths.

"Namaste, Ravi," replied the priest, adjusting his shawl. "You never come to the temple, do you?" The priest asked curiously, hoping to know how someone's celebration could be complete without visiting the temple.

Ravidas simply smiled and didn't say anything. The priest however couldn't contain himself and continued, "It is sad that you've never stepped into the house of God. Have you never felt the desire to see Him or seek His blessings?"

Ravi's smile deepened, but he remained silent. This irked the priest, who muttered under his breath as he hurried towards the temple, "What does this cobbler know of God? No wonder he spends his life in the dirt, mending smelly shoes."

All through the day, the priest was unable to forget Ravidas' smiling face that continued to linger in his thoughts. He was totally upset by the fact that someone could be happy and contented without visiting the temple or engaging in rituals. His entire life he had been preaching that God held the key to happiness and the temple was His home. All good things in life were supposed to come through this. But Ravidas' smile, free from the burden of rituals, seemed to mock the redundancy of it all. The priest's frustration grew, and by evening, he resolved to 'enlighten' the cobbler.

In the evening, while he passed by Ravi's house, he saw he was already asleep. The priest, who was already upset by the morning incident, shook his head in disbelief. "It is only eight o'clock in the evening, and this guy is asleep! So lazy! It is my moral duty to awaken him not just from his sleep but also from his ignorance. He needs to awaken to the purpose of his life before his lazy ways spread to the whole town. I can't allow a man's potential to go waste like that."

Determined, the priest knocked loudly on Ravidas' door until the cobbler woke up. Rubbing his eyes, Ravidas welcomed the priest with a calm demeanour. "Panditji, what brings you here at this hour?"

"Ravi," the priest spoke in an earnest tone, "As a temple priest, I feel it is my duty to look after the well being of the town people. Your lifestyle is alarming and I am really concerned about it. I see that you do not worship God and this could bring trouble into your life. You must cleanse yourself of sins and invite divine blessings into your home, for your own good."

Ravidas listened intently and asked, "What must I do to cleanse myself, Panditji?"

The priest straightened, pleased with the question. "First, you must fast. Eat only fruits to purify your body and soul."

Ravidas chuckled softly. "But, Panditji, I already eat only fruits every day."

The priest hesitated but quickly continued. "Then you must light a lamp in your house each evening to drive away the darkness."

"But, Panditji," Ravidas replied, "The sun lights my house by day, and the moon and stars by night. Is that not enough?"

The priest grew agitated and thought he must scare Ravi by instilling fear of evil in him. So he went on to say "Do you know if you don't visit the temple or worship God, evil spirits will haunt you in the dark?"

At this Ravi laughed. "'Yes, Panditji, I can see it—you're absolutely right. The spirit is right here, haunting me now!" He said pointing playfully at the priest.

The priest froze for a moment, embarrassed at the absurdity of his own words firing back at him. He realized it wasn't Ravidas who needed enlightenment but himself. Flustered, he mumbled something incoherent and left, leaving Ravidas smiling quietly in the stillness of the night.

Flight of Freedom

"A bird, whether in hand or in the bush,

Lives best when free"

On the outskirts of the village of Baandi, stood a small, timeworn temple. Deserted and neglected, its crumbling walls seemed to echo the villagers' fading interest in the Divine. Each morning, the sun's rays filtered through the temple's eaves and brackets, playing with motes of dust on the abandoned idols, only to retreat by dusk. The temple stood silently, waiting for a visitor—someone who might restore its lost glory.

As days turned into months, the ageing temple grew weary of its solitude. Weakened by years of neglect, and unable to offer rituals in worship, it silently prayed on behalf of the villagers who had once entrusted it with their faith.

One fine morning, as the sun sent its golden beams through the temple, an old fakir arrived. He had been walking all night through the forest, with the hope of finding a village where he could rest and find some food. Relieved to see the temple, he stepped inside. The sight of its derelict state tugged at his heart. Even though he was tired he decided not to rest until he had cleaned the temple. Resolute, he set to work, pouring his energy into restoring its dignity. The temple, infused with

21

the fakir's enthusiasm, seemed to spring back to life, with the care of its long-awaited visitor.

Passers-by, noticing the refreshed temple, brought the fakir fruits and sweets as tokens of gratitude. He thanked the Divine for rewarding his labor and reaffirming his belief that no effort goes unnoticed.

After a meal and a bath in the nearby pond, the fakir wandered through the village. What he saw startled him: nearly every household had caged birds. Some homes boasted a single bird, while others housed dozens in ornately decorated cages. Bird-catching and cage-making were evidently the lifeblood of the village economy.

As he rested under a tree near a bird-catcher's home, the fakir's attention was drawn to two birds in a cage—a parrot and a cockatoo—engaged in conversation.

"Don't you ever wish to escape this cage?" the parrot asked.

The cockatoo replied, "Escape? What for? In the jungle, I spent my days struggling to find food, building nests, and dodging predators. Here, I sleep in peace, food is served, and our master keeps us safe. Plus we have this luxurious cage to stay in. I am so much enjoying this! Who wants to be free when life is so easy here?"

The parrot was taken aback by the cockatoo's words. He fell silent for a while with his thoughts in turmoil. He had grown up hearing tales about the boundless joy of freedom, passed down by his elders as sacred truths. All those tales, knit into family values and beliefs, glorified freedom as the most precious asset for a bird. But here was this cockatoo, who spoke from direct experience. His words seemed true and convincing too. Now the parrot, torn between his own set of ideals and the words of the cockatoo, began to question everything he had been taught. "Is freedom truly as precious as I believed, or is it a burden masked as a virtue? While the cockatoo enjoys his stay here, is my sadness, about being caged, born of clinging to outdated ideals?" He asked himself.

"What the cockatoo says is exactly the opposite of my own beliefs, but they are convincing as they are powered by direct experience. My beliefs lack power as they lack experience. They were simply passed down from generation to generation and maybe those who passed me those beliefs were themselves struggling against them internally. Maybe they too wished for an easy life and hated the struggles of a life that was free, but not exactly free. Then what exactly is freedom? *If simply being out of the cage isn't freedom, then what is it?"*

The fakir, overhearing this exchange, sensed the parrot's inner conflict. He rose and knocked on the bird-catcher's door. A child's voice inside pleaded, "Father, please set the birds free!"

The father responded, "Nonsense! They're safe here. If I set them free, a cat will eat them in no time."

The fakir smiled and addressed the bird-catcher, "Would you sell me that cage with the two birds? I'll pay a good price."

The bird-catcher, delighted by the offer, readily agreed. The fakir handed over all the money he had collected in alms and carried the cage back to the temple. Once there, he opened the cage. The birds hesitated, stepping out cautiously. They did not fly. Years of captivity had dulled their instincts with a dependant mind-set and atrophied their wings. They had forgotten how to fly. They had no idea where to go, where to find food. They looked to the fakir for guidance.

The fakir knowingly scattered some grains a short distance away from them. The birds waddled towards the food, and were exhausted by the small effort. The fakir understood they had forgotten what it meant to be birds. He decided to help them rediscover their essence.

The fakir knew that flying was instinctive in birds, and was confident that one day they would surely fly. Over the days, the birds roamed freely within the temple. They watched the fakir perform his rituals, they ate when he ate, and rested when he rested. The birds started feeling at home in the temple and the fakir seemed like family to them. Moving about they felt much healthier and now they focused more on learning and exploring things than on food and comfort. Gradually their limbs grew stronger and short flights turned into longer ones; boosting their confidence. They could now fly, perch upon the trees and search their own food and water. But even as they were quite independent, fear had not left their hearts. They knew they were safe in the temple, but beyond that, it was an unknown world!

Knowing that *extreme situations bring out the best in individuals*, the fakir introduced a cat into the temple to push them further. Startled upon being chased by the cat, the birds took a magnificent flight, soaring higher than they ever had before. They were frightened when they took off, but were exhilarated to realize that they landed on the highest branch of the tallest tree in the courtyard! Even though trembling as they landed; elated, they smiled at each other.

 "Until now I had viewed cats as enemies --- enemies that were meant to be feared, to be despised, and to stay away from. But today I realized, that what had always appeared to be a threat; became our propellant to strength!" said the cockatoo.

 "Indeed, *if we face our fears we become stronger*, "added the parrot.

"Escaping the cat obviously made us feel stronger, but what if we were caught and feasted upon by the cat?" asked the cockatoo.

"Even then, our entire being would have continued to live as part of a stronger animal" replied the parrot with a newfound understanding. "Death as we have known and feared, is no longer the same to me. I realize *that existence is designed to support evolution, not fear.* So let's fly fearlessly and for the joy it brings."

"You mean, true freedom isn't just about finding one's food and escaping enemies?" The cockatoo asked.

"Indeed, true freedom means freedom from fear, where enemies are not viewed as enemies, but as opportunities to evolve into stronger and better versions of ourselves. It is one that opens a vast world, of infinite possibilities to be explored" replied the parrot, having realized that true freedom wasn't the mere absence of a cage. "It's a freedom that widens horizons and broadens the vision! This freedom brings joy, a sense of wonder and amazement for simply being alive in this world! This is the freedom I had always believed in, whose tales I had heard from my elders. And now it is powered by my own experience!" He could clearly feel the difference between experience and belief, and concluded "I understand now that our beliefs come from experience, but the reverse could also be made true."

From that day, flying became their daily practice. They flew not just for survival but for the sheer joy of it. They discovered landscapes from new heights and marveled at the vastness of the world.

The cockatoo also understood the value of true freedom. One day as they sat resting after a long flight, the cockatoo said, "Earlier I didn't realize that even in the comfort of the cage, death was inevitable. But now when I look back, I feel, life in the cage was a mere cyclic repetition of feeding, excreting and sleeping! It lacked the essence of flight. The security offered by the cage was a dependant security; food availability and safety were subject to the master. We weren't secure, we were simply dependent. Now I understand that true security comes from self-reliance and fearlessness. True freedom is true security, as it awakens the master within us. It's the master who sets you free to fly!" The parrot smiled at the invaluable learning the cockatoo shared. His experience, that had powered his beliefs earlier, was replaced by a greater experience!

"I'm glad you understood that a true master is not one who feeds you in a cage for his own amusement, but one who sets you free and helps you overcome your limitations. One who helps you understand true freedom and helps you discover that true security is not just about being in a 'safe' place but in overcoming fears."

The birds flew high and for once returned to thank the fakir for releasing them and bringing them to this realization. As they sat perched on his shoulders, the fakir said to them: *"God made a bird of himself, not for food, or to run away from enemies, but to fly. So fly and let God fly through you. May you be one with Him as you fly."*

Then the cockatoo asked "But what about the other birds like us, who are caged?"

To this the fakir replied: **"***Fly with fervour, fly with passion and fly with joy... and your joy shall make them seek their own.***"**

With this, the fakir set on his journey once again. His work in the temple was complete now. More temples in other villages awaited him...

A Letter to God

When I was eight, my mother had been unwell for days. I remember sitting by her bedside, holding her hand, and asking my father, "When will Mummy get better?"

He paused for a moment, then said with a smile, "If you write a letter to God and ask Him to make Mummy well, she'll recover soon. God answers children's prayers very quickly."

Taking him at his word, I rushed to my room, tore a page from my notebook, and began writing. "Dear God," I scrawled in my childish handwriting, "Please make my mummy better. She is very nice, and I love her a lot." I added little drawings of flowers and hearts, carefully colouring them with my crayons, hoping to make the letter special enough for God to notice.

"Papa, I need a stamp." I said, holding up my masterpiece.

He smiled. "Letters to God don't need stamps. Just fold it and address it to Him."

I folded the paper into a neat rectangle, wrote TO GOD in big letters on the front, and glued the edges like an inland letter. I then ran to the red post-box near our house and slid the letter in. As I walked back home, I kept thinking if the letter would really reach God? But in my heart I prayed and hoped it would.

For the next two weeks, every time I heard the postman's bicycle bell, I would run towards the gate, hoping for a reply. But the reply never came as a letter. One morning, I noticed Mummy smiling as she sat up in bed. Her strength was slowly returning. I was happy to see her recover and felt that God had finally answered me.

As time passed, I stopped thinking about the letter or waiting for a reply. But a question remained unanswered in my mind: who was this God I had written to? I had heard people speak of Him often, but I couldn't see Him, hear Him, or talk to Him, the way I could with the people around me. To me, God was some distant being, residing in some far off heaven.

Slowly as life paced on, the search for this answer went into the background. Yet, whenever I heard someone talk about God, it would stir in me the desire to know God. For once in my lifetime, I wanted to meet Him, know Him and see what He looked like.

Four years later, during a school seminar, I found an opportunity to ask. The seminar was led by Father Ivo Fernandez, the head priest of the local church. He was someone I supposed would have some sort of connection with God. When he spoke about God, I raised my hand. "Father," I said, "Have you ever seen God? Everyone talks about Him, but I've never seen Him. Is there a way by which it is possible for me to see Him?"

Father Ivo smiled gently. "Do you know how butter is hidden in milk?" he asked.

"Hmm, yes," I replied hesitantly.

"It's there, but you can't see it until the milk is churned. God is also like that—He's present in the world, but seems invisible to the inexperienced eye. To see Him, you must churn your thoughts."

I nodded, but the answer didn't fully satisfy me. "Butter, after all, becomes visible at some point. Why couldn't God?" I thought as the seminar moved on, and my question remained unanswered.

Seeing God seemed like an eternal mystery, solving which was something I didn't know how to go about at the time.

Over the years, I met people with all kinds of beliefs—atheists, theists, agnostics, and fanatics. I also read a wide range of books that offered diverse perspectives on spirituality. Each encounter broadened my vision, brought deeper insights and added a new layer to my understanding. Yet the mystery of God persisted.

Then one day, years later, I had a conversation with my son. We were sitting in the park, looking up at the sky. "What do you think about God?" I asked, curious to hear his thoughts.

He looked at me and replied, *"Maa, God isn't a distant being sitting in a far-off heaven, as you believe. God is very ordinary, found everywhere. I see God in everything."*

His reply amazed me; I looked at him, wondering at his innocence and clarity of thought. How simply he had answered the question that had taken me decades to understand. His simple reply unravelled the vision; I had yearned for years, in an instant.

I looked back in time, comparing his views to mine at his age. It had been a long journey—from believing in a God in a far-off heaven to finding Him everywhere. I realized it wasn't about what you see, but how you choose to see that truly matters.

The Gods of Two Hands

Rahul and his mother were returning from the temple, where he had seen the four-armed idol of Lord Vishnu seated serenely on the coiled throne of a serpent. Visiting the temple was a daily routine, but today felt different. As they were leaving, the priest had handed Rahul a flower with a warm smile.

"This is a blessing from Lord Vishnu," the priest had said. "Keep it with you, and he will always protect you."

Rahul took the flower but his young mind was filled with questions. "How can a stone idol protect me? It just stays in the temple, unmoved. If I ever fall and scrape my knee, how would it come to heal me? And If I am tired and need some loving care to forget the pain and sleep in peace, how would it come to soothe me and put me to sleep? If I am hungry or crave chocolates, would it be able to provide me food and chocolates?" He pondered deeply on the priest's words as he walked back home.

His mother noticed that he was quieter than usual but didn't say anything. She let him find his way through his thoughts. Finally, when Rahul couldn't hold back any longer, he tugged at her hand, and asked, "Maa, Lord Vishnu has four arms, right? But he just sits there in the temple. He doesn't move or do anything. Everyone says he protects and helps us, but I've never seen him do anything."

His mother smiled, sensing the curiosity bubbling within him.

"Daddy only has two arms," Rahul continued, "but he goes to work every day and takes care of us. And you—you work hard around the house, keeping it clean, cooking nutritious meals and taking care of me. I feel safe and loved because you both are always around. But I've never seen Lord Vishnu around. He just stays on his throne in the temple."

Seeing Rahul trying to understand things, his mother bent down to his level and gently cupped his face in her hand. "You're asking good questions, Rahul," she said with a smile, "We are all manifestations of God. The idol in the temple reminds us of God's qualities, but his real presence is in the goodness we show and the love we give. You're right—your father and I are always here for you. Maybe you're too young to understand this fully, but one day, you will."

Rahul, unable to comprehend her words completely, remained unsatisfied with her answer. He watched her head to the kitchen to prepare dinner, while he remained outside, lost in thought.

He felt unenthused to play with his friends that day and sat in the garden, brooding. He silently watched the birds flying past, the butterflies fluttering over the flowers, and the squirrels leaping from tree to tree. Usually, he'd be chasing them in glee, but today he sat still, while his mind went hopping from question to question like the squirrels.

The sun dipped behind the trees, painting the sky in shades of orange and purple. The cool evening breeze ruffled his hair, but Rahul barely noticed. His thoughts kept circling back to the same question: where was God in his life?

The sound of the doorbell startled him, breaking his reverie. His father had returned from work.

Suddenly a thought lit up in Rahul's mind, and a small smile spread across his face. He hurried to the garden, plucking a handful of flowers. His mother watched curiously as he darted past her, with flowers in his hand.

"Rahul, what are you up to?" she asked, but he didn't answer.

Rahul rushed to his father, who had just settled into his chair. Grabbing his hand, he said eagerly, 'Come, Daddy, sit here,' guiding him to the sofa at the center of the room. His mother followed, puzzled, as Rahul motioned for her to sit beside his father.

"What's going on?" his father asked, amused. "Did you see a new toy you want?"

Rahul shook his head, his face was serious but his eyes glowed with understanding. He brought his hands forward, revealing the flowers he had been hiding. Gently, he placed them at his parents' feet, just as he had seen his mother do at the temple each morning and bowed at their feet to seek blessings.

His parents exchanged a surprised glance as Rahul knelt before them, and spoke with a warm innocence in his voice. "I don't know if the four-handed God in the temple is real, or not. I've only seen his statue, but I know two gods who have two hands each—and they are as real as me. They're here for me, everyday; protecting me, loving me, and making me feel safe. Together, both of you make my four-handed Vishnu."

His mother's eyes moistened while his father smiled with pride. He pulled Rahul into a hug.

Rahul had finally found an answer that satisfied him. He realized that the four handed God lived in the temple of his home ---- in the care, sacrifice and love of his parents. Nestled in their embrace, he felt closer to God than ever before.

The Real Buddha

A Zen monastery stood in silence, shaded by an ancient willow tree, its roots caressing a clear stream that bubbled over smooth pebbles before merging with a distant river. Like a Zen monk, the river moved dispassionately away from its banks, flowing toward unknown lands. The afternoon sun warmed the winter chill, and a playful wind rustled the willow's branches, sending leaves drifting like tiny boats across the emerald waters.

Nearby, a shepherd boy led his flock to graze on the lush green pastures. While his sheep drank from the stream, he lay on the grass, soaking in the sun's warmth. His tranquil rest was soon interrupted by the soft shuffle of footsteps. Sitting up, he saw Zen monks wearing maroon robes walking toward the monastery. Intrigued, he watched them disappear inside.

Later, on his way back, as he passed the monastery, his curiosity drew him to a window. Inside, he saw a serene statue of Buddha in deep meditation, surrounded by monks offering fruits and delicacies at its feet. The sight filled him with wonder. "So many fruits! Such delicious food!" he thought. "Tomorrow, I'll have lunch with Buddha!" But waiting until tomorrow made him restless. That night, he tossed and turned in his bed, his excitement keeping him awake. His mother woke from the noise and chided him for being fidgety, but he silently held on to his dreams of the next day.

At dawn, he sprang from bed, eager to begin his adventure. Leaving his flock in a friend's care, he rushed to the temple in the monastery. Inside, he sat near the Buddha statue, closing his eyes like the monks. He waited patiently for the Buddha to take the first bite from the offerings. As time passed, he couldn't resist peeking, but found that Buddha's eyes were still closed, and he hadn't even touched the food. Morning turned to afternoon, and his hunger grew. Still, Buddha didn't move. Exhausted and famished, the boy fell asleep at the statue's feet.

A monk found him there and gently woke him. "Child, why are you sleeping here?" the monk asked.

"I was waiting for Buddha to open his eyes and share a meal with me," the boy replied.

The monk smiled kindly. "That's not the real Buddha, my boy. It's just a statue."

The words struck the boy like lightning. "If this isn't the real Buddha, then where is he?" he wondered.

The question consumed him and he sat still, thinking deeply. Then he asked the monk, "If this statue isn't Buddha, what makes all the monks to bow to it? If Buddha isn't just a body of stone, then he isn't merely a body of flesh either. So the person, who was the Buddha, had something more than merely a body. What is it that makes someone a Buddha?"

The monk smiled and said, "The real Buddha is within each one of us. He is in you, in this awareness that you are more than just your body."

The boy looked at the monk in amazement, as he listened to this profound truth and awakened to the presence of the life within himself.

Elements

Om Prithvi Namah

(I Bow to the Mother Earth)

"That which nourishes the seed;
Grows and evolves with it"

Filmmaking had always been Diksha's passion. Her camera was a window to untold stories, taking her to places the world needed to see. One such journey brought her to an ancient tribal village nestled deep in the hills of North-Eastern India.

The raw countryside untouched by modernity captivated Diksha by its earthy charm. The lush green fields and winding clean lanes lined with aromatic herbs, hummed with life and the unhurried rhythm of life flowing gently, lent a tranquil aura to the place. What struck her most was the villagers' profound connection with the Earth.

Reverence for the Earth was entwined in their daily lifestyle. The people there walked barefoot, not out of poverty, but out of reverence for the Earth. The sight reminded Diksha of the chaotic, rushing feet at the metro stations in Mumbai, which seemed a stark contrast to these gentle, mindful strides, grounded in awareness of the contact they made with the Earth.

Curious to learn more, Diksha approached a group of farmers tending their fields. "Namaste, I'm new here and already in love with your village. It's beautiful," she said with a smile. "It feels so clean and peaceful here. How do you keep it this way?"

A middle-aged farmer paused, wiping sweat from his brow. "The credit goes to our chief," he said with a warm smile. "He reminds us that we are children of the soil. Like a mother, the Earth feeds us, nourishes us and watches us grow. When we plant crops on the fields, we see Mother Earth ascending and rising and sacrificing herself after a full grown harvest to feed us. When we are old and weary, she embraces us, and takes us in her lap for a much needed rest. We owe her respect and make sure that she is clean and happy."

Another farmer added, "Every home here has a temple for Mother Earth. We start our day by offering her flowers. And we never let waste pile up; it's all composted or reused. Even our cooking fuel comes from biogas. It's really simple, when you care for the Earth, she cares for you."

Diksha was fascinated. "It's really amazing" she said. "But where does this inspiration come from?"

"You should meet our chief," one of the farmers replied. "He's usually out with his sheep around this time. You'll find him near the eastern fields."

Diksha thanked the farmers as she left. Eager to explore more, she wandered through the village, where she noticed women decorating their thresholds with *rangolis*, drawn with rice flour, turmeric and flowers. They welcomed her to join them.

"These *rangolis* are beautiful; do you make them every day?" Diksha asked, kneeling beside one of them.

"It's our way of adorning Mother Earth," a woman explained. "We see Mother Earth as a householder. She works tirelessly, sweeping her home with winds, lighting it with the sun, and cooking veggies and fruits in its warmth. She doesn't need walls or roofs as she has to allow the rains to fill up ponds and streams. Tending her endless garden with carpets of greens, she's set up a food chain as her pest control!"

The ladies laughed with an infectious joy as they spoke.

Another woman added, "She's an independent woman, handling all this on her own and she seems to enjoy it! We can feel her happiness expressed through our flourishing farms and livestock. She doesn't even see this as selfless service, because, to her, we are part of her—her own Self." She is our inspiration and we try to live by her example."

Diksha smiled as she listened to them. She felt a sense of peace she hadn't known in a long time. She thanked the women and made her way to meet the chief.

She found him on a dirt path, leading a flock of sheep. He danced joyfully as he walked, and the flock swayed to his rhythm behind him.

As she approached, he stopped and greeted her warmly. "Ah, you must be the filmmaker everyone's been talking about," he said smiling warmly.

Diksha introduced herself and expressed her admiration for the village. "Your teachings have shaped a beautiful way of life here," she said.

The chief smiled humbly. "It's not my teaching; it's Mother Earth's. She shows us that everything—living and non-living—comes from her. She nourishes us, shelters us, and asks for nothing in return. To her, we are part of her, just as a fruit is part of the tree."

He bent down, picked a ripe watermelon, and handed it to Diksha. "Here, hold this," he said.

She took it, surprised by its weight.

"It feels heavy, doesn't it?" he asked. Diksha nodded, her arms straining slightly. "But once you've eaten it—made it a part of yourself—it's no longer a burden, isn't it?" he said with a twinkle in his eyes. "That's how the Earth sees us—not as burden to carry, but as a part of herself."

Diksha smiled, moved by his simple yet profound wisdom.

As she walked back to her lodging, she reflected on everything she had seen and heard. The hurried, crowded streets of Mumbai faded from her memory; replaced by the beautiful, serene earthy lanes of the village.

That night, as she reviewed her footage, Diksha felt a quiet joy. She softly repeated the mantra of the villagers to herself, *"Om Prithvi Namah."*

She had come to document the village through her camera lens, but the village gifted her something far greater - a new lens to view the world through the eyes of the Earth.

Om Vrikshaya Namah

(I Bow to the Trees)

India is a country where people worship anything from stones, trees, rivers, stars, planets or even snakes. The ancient principle that *'the divine pervades all'* is practiced quite literally here, though at times, certain practices may appear contradictory.

I lived in the small town of Ambala, located in North India, for over twenty years. Life there was slower than in bustling metros but had its own charm. I remember visiting the temple near my house on Sunday mornings and Tuesday evenings. The stone idols inside were bathed in milk and adorned with the most delicious sweets, dressed in attractive costumes with carefully matched accessories. Outside, however, sat a beggar in tattered clothes, rarely receiving more than a meagre serving of *prasad* to eat. This stark contrast between the lifeless stone idols within the temple and the living tramp outside often made me think it was better to be a stone idol than a human in need. Yet, the entire community accepted this practice without question—no objections, no arguments, just peace with the process.

Although this disparity unsettled me, the rituals themselves brought a sense of calm I couldn't explain. At that time, I didn't understand their meaning, but I cherished the peace they brought. Outside the temple stood a grand *Peepal* tree, around which sari-clad women lit lamps, burned camphor and incense, tied threads, and bowed in reverence. Often, a few crows would perch on its branches, cawing as though chanting a mantra. As a child, I often wondered, "Why so much for a tree? It's just a tree!" Back then, I thought trees were lifeless, much like the stones around us.

Years later when I moved to Nabha, I met another majestic *Peepal* just opposite my new home. Hundreds of birds lived on this tree and their chirpings became my morning wake up call.

Each morning the owner of the house would scatter grains and fill a bowl of water for the birds to drink. It was a joy to watch the birds eat the grain and sip water from the bowl. At times they would even bathe in it! The owner and his wife were simple people, who loved and respected nature as a way of life. They had planted many trees and had a small farm near the house. As a daily ritual after feeding the birds, they would light incense to worship the trees. From them I learned that love and respect for Nature is not just an occasional activity rather a part of our daily lives that brings peace as we live in harmony with it.

One day the serenity of the place was shattered by the clatter of heavy chains, outside the house. As I went over to have a look, my heart sank. The grand *Peepal* tree was being pulled down. A contractor had bought the land and was clearing space for an upcoming building. The birds flitted around frantically, their cries piercing the air, as if pleading for their sanctuary to be spared. The whole scene was so upsetting; I could hardly stand any longer to watch. The grand *Peepal,* that had been a home to so many lives and had offered shade and solace to innumerable travellers since years, was being pulled down, and we could do nothing about it. It was hard to believe that the next day we wouldn't see it any more. Despite its resistance, it fell, its silent pleas unheard by those wielding the machines. It took two days of relentless digging and pulling to bring it down. I wondered if it cried for help, though its voice was beyond our audible range. But do trees need a voice? They trust us to be their voice, yet we remain deaf to their plight. How can we be so heartless?

In days that followed, the place seemed to burn in the scorching sun with its emptiness echoing the absence of the *Peepal* tree. The birds nostalgically revisited the place, though their usual chirpiness was replaced by a gloomy silence.

This incident brought me back to the *Peepal* tree outside the temple in Ambala, and I finally understood why it was worshipped. Trees are extraordinary beings, spending their entire lives moving towards light, carrying the multitude of cells within them from the darkness of ignorance to enlightenment. They embody compassion and forgiveness, offering sanctuary even to the insects that bore holes into their trunks—qualities we often pride ourselves on as humans, yet trees portray this so effortlessly. They provide nesting grounds to countless birds, willingly accepting even their droppings. Perhaps this acceptance turns them into fertilizers. They even welcome snakes in the hollows of their trunks and don't mind squirrels scurrying about their branches.

Like a nurturing parent, a tree selflessly supports an entire ecosystem, thriving on its generosity. It consumes the dirt of the soil and transforms it into nourishing fruits, serving as sustenance for others. Beyond that, their noble service extends to cleansing the air, inhaling toxic fumes and exhaling life-giving oxygen. Even after death, a tree continues to give, providing wood for homes and hearths. Above all, trees are profound teachers, imparting invaluable life lessons in their own silent, ways—simply by being themselves.

It was so ignorant of me to have thought 'why so much for a tree?' In fact, trees deserve much more. Worshipping trees is the least we can do, but what they truly need is our protection—so their silent wisdom can continue to guide generations to come.

Om Samudraya Namah

(I Bow to the Ocean)

Life is an endless journey of learning. Everywhere we look, there are lessons waiting to be discovered. If we awaken the learner within us, the whole world can become our teacher.

It was a sunny December afternoon when my family and I visited the seaside at Cherating, Malaysia. The vast, endless ocean stretched before us, with waves wrinkling upon its sun kissed waters. As I strolled along the shore, I saw the ocean as a wise old man, who had stood there since ages. It had endured the storms of time and had been a witness to the years gone by. Its waves flowing in an eternal rhythm seemed rich with ancient, timeless stories of wisdom. I felt it had much to share and I was ready to listen.

Here's what I got to learn from the wise old ocean:

Humility
As the waves lapped at my feet and gently washed them, I was reminded of a ritual my father performed every year during *kanyapujan* – a ceremony conducted on the eighth day of Navratri. He would wash the feet of little girls, honouring them as living embodiments of the Divine Mother and seek her blessings.

Standing there, I felt a similar blessing emanating from my heart for the ocean. I was touched by the humility coming from its vastness, with its waves kneeling before me, offering silent ablutions. In that moment, the ocean appeared as a vast liquid temple, purifying me before I entered its sacred precincts.

Modesty

Just days earlier, we had visited a gem factory displaying treasures of the ocean—pearls, corals, and other rare jewels extracted from its depths. Now, as I looked at the unassuming ocean surface, I marveled at its modesty.

Despite its hidden riches, the ocean felt no need to flaunt its treasures. Its vast, unfathomable form spoke for itself. This quiet modesty taught me that true greatness doesn't seek recognition—it simply is.

Unimpressed and Majestic

As I walked along the shore, I noticed how the ocean erased every footprint in the sand, leaving no trace of those who had walked before. Water, by its nature, remains unimpressed, as if reminding us of the impermanence of human efforts. Even when we step on it, the marks disappear as soon as we move on.

Like a sage in meditation, the ocean seemed detached, content in its vast existence, playing with its waves without seeking attention. It reminded me of the futility of striving to leave an impression and the value of simply being—content and complete within oneself.

Vast yet Within Limits

Despite covering seventy percent of the planet, the ocean respects its boundaries. It is interesting that even though we have divided this vast expanse of water and named it differently as the Pacific, Atlantic and Indian oceans, the ocean itself doesn't recognize these borders. Yet it stays true to the natural limits set for it.

It doesn't encroach on the land, and the land, in turn, honours the space of the ocean. This mutual respect for healthy natural boundaries seems to reflect the nature of its self-discipline, respecting its limits and valuing the need of coexistence.

Acceptance

Looking at the ocean, my thoughts wandered to the journey of water—the glaciers melting in the mountains, rivers flowing through dusty plains, even polluted streams from crowded cities—all eventually find their way to the ocean.

The ocean accepts everything that flows into it, without judgment or resistance. It transforms even the dirtiest water, cleansing and recycling it into something new, renewing it through the endless cycle of nature. This all-welcoming attitude made me realize the power of acceptance, of embracing life's experiences, both good and bad, with equanimity and trust in the power of the self to transform it.

A Friend Who Embraces and Uplifts

As I stood watching the waves roll in, an amazing thought struck me - 'every *drop of water that flows to the ocean never falls further*'. It has only two options, either it stays there or it rises. So the ocean *either makes you one with itself or it uplifts you, it doesn't let you fall again. Like a good* friend, it embraces you, accepting you as you are, supports you when you're down by being with you and even provides a ground for you to rise higher.

This made me smile. What a beautiful reminder to be that kind of friend—one who never lets others fall further but instead helps them find their ground or soar.

A Great Teacher

The sea taught me all of this without a single word. Its presence was its lesson. As I walked away from the shore, I realized that life itself is like the ocean. We can choose to stand at the edge, letting its waves touch us, or dive deep inside to explore its treasures or sail across it to discover our own strengths. The choice is ours.

As I turned back for one last look, my heart bowed in gratitude to this great teacher, whispering, *"Om Samudraya Namah"*.

Om Agni Namah

(I Bow to the Element of Fire)

For over twenty years of their married life, Mr. and Mrs. Sharma had followed a cherished routine of visiting the temple each evening. The walk to the temple and the lighting of a *diya* there, were symbolic of their sacred journey to enlightenment.

 Mr. Sharma believed there was a certain mystical quality in the light of a *diya's* flame which he found missing in electric lamps. "The flame of a diya is unique," he would say, "it has an aliveness which is a perfect blend of discipline and freedom, something you cannot find in the glass bound glow of electric lamps."

Agni, the sacred fire, held special significance for him. He often reflected on the day of his wedding, when he and his wife had taken their vows with *Agni* as their witness. Since then, the worship of *Agni* in yagyas - the fire sacrifices had become an integral part of his life. It meant to him much more than a ritual. He dived deep into their symbolism to connect them with his way of life.

Their neighbor, Daya, wasn't much inclined toward rituals, but he often found himself drawn to the warmth and serenity of the Sharmas' practices. Whenever he saw Mr. Sharma perform an *Agni yagya*, he felt a strange pull of curiosity. One evening, as the Sharmas performed a *yagya*, Mr. Sharma noticed Daya observing them inquisitively, peering over the wall between their houses. Seeing his interest and eagerness, Mr Sharma invited him to attend the ceremony. "Daya ji, come over and join us," he said warmly.

Daya hesitated a bit at first, but then went over to sit with them. He observed attentively as Mr. Sharma prepared for the ritual. With meticulous care, he built a vedi, a square altar of bricks and sand, adorning it with turmeric, vermilion, and wheat flour, drawing signs of the sun, moon, and planets to invoke their presence and blessings for the ritual. Dry mango twigs were stacked neatly, camphor placed to ignite the fire, and a mango leaf spoon readied for pouring ghee into the flames.

As the sacred fire was ignited, Mr. Sharma chanted Vedic mantras, offering ghee, milk, sesame seeds, honey and a mixture of herbs, nuts and coconut into the sacred fire. The ritual intended to nourish – *Agni*, the prime deity of the ceremony. The air filled with the fragrant smoke of the yagya, seemed to transform the atmosphere around. When the yagya concluded, Daya, visibly curious, asked, "All this seems so symbolic. I'd like to know the meaning behind all this symbolism. What does it signify and is it really relevant in today's world?"

Mr. Sharma smiled. "It's absolutely symbolic but also deeply practical," he explained. "The Fire element is a tremendous phenomenon of Nature. It represents our digestive fire, our internal *Agni.* Just as we light the yagya fire before offering oblations, we should awaken our hunger before eating. When we eat without true hunger, it's like offering materials into a weak flame—it leads to sluggishness and extinguishes the flame of vitality. But when the digestive fire is kindled properly, it sustains us, keeping us active and brilliant, like a well-fed flame."

Daya listened intently. Mr. Sharma continued, "And then there's the funeral pyre. That's a different kind of fire altogether. In this case, the offering—our physical body—is placed first, and *Agni* follows, consuming what's no longer needed. It's a symbolic act of purification, burning away accumulated waste and completing the cycle of life. The exercises we do to get rid of unwanted excess are also a kind of purification fire ritual. Creation by nourishing the fire and purification by allowing the fire to remove the excess, both are essential for life."

Fascinated, Daya gestured toward the diyas in the temple. "And the flames of these lamps?"

"These flames remind us of the light within," replied Mr. Sharma, gently touching the sides of his forehead. "These temples in our bodies denote the seat of the mind, a sacred space – the gateway to the soul, which is why we call them temples. Lighting a diya is symbolic of lighting the lamp of awakening, igniting the light of self-awareness within. It reminds us to walk the path of knowledge, to move from the darkness of ignorance toward the light of clarity. And if you have noticed, a flame always moves upwards, its very nature is illuminating and uplifting."

As the evening deepened, Mr. Sharma shared more wisdom about *Agni*. "Fire is a great equalizer. It burns without bias. Whether you offer gold or trash into it, fire burns them indiscriminately, but reveals their true essence in the process. Similarly, suffering doesn't discriminate; it touches everyone irrespective of status or wealth. But in the fire of suffering, we see who we truly are. Some by nature are like the incense, releasing the fragrance of wisdom. Others release fumes of anger and yet others may let out the smoke of blames and complaints."

Daya nodded thoughtfully. "And what about the fire in Hindu wedding ceremonies?" he asked, recalling Mr. Sharma's earlier mention of wedding vows.

"Ah, the wedding fire!" Mr. Sharma chuckled. "Marriage is a union of souls, much like *Agni* unites elements to create something new. Think of rice and water. They remain separate until they're cooked over fire. Only then they unite and transform into a nourishing meal. Marriage is similar. The fire of love, desire, and commitment blends two lives into one. Sometimes it's a slow simmer; other times, it's a roaring flame. But transformation is inevitable."

As the night settled, Daya went home and lit a lamp. He smiled looking at the flame, with reverence, as if a small light had kindled within him and in his heart he chanted the mantra, *"Om Agni Namah."*

Om Vayu Namah

(I Bow to the Element of Air)

Years ago I started my kriya-yoga practice. The word kriya means action and yoga means union. The practice aims at becoming one with our action in such a way that it becomes an inseparable part of our identity and flows through us effortlessly, just like the life within us is fluent in the act of breathing.

As part of the practice, we engaged in pranayama—a breathing exercise designed to cultivate awareness of breath. This exercise made me view the air around me in a new light. I observed that although invisible, air is indispensable for sustaining life. Even though it is vital for our survival, air never asserts its presence. This made me ponder on the importance we place on being visible in our lives. I felt that those who genuinely understand the value of their work and contributions to the world will neither assert their presence nor resent being invisible.

The more I practiced the pranayama the more aware I became of my breath. It led me to discover that we breathe not only with our respiratory organs, but with our entire body. We may not notice it often, but we also breathe through our skin. You might notice that wearing tight clothing can feel constricting because our skin loses its freedom to breathe. Our entire body is enveloped by *Vayu* – the air element. Restricting its flow makes us conscious of the profound connection between our body and breath.

The practice of conscious breathing had a transformative, two-way effect. Breathing consciously heightened my awareness, and this awareness, in turn, helped me improve upon my breathing. I came to see that the air within us is just as powerful as the air around us. It is a force of movement and an energy catalyst for life itself. With each inhalation we breathe in life and vitality, and with every exhalation we infuse the world with our energy, making our world come alive.

It was through observing breath carefully that I found it is in its nature to live and let live. Breath is a unique and miraculous rhythm that nurtures both the self and others equally, without seeking anything in return. Breath gives selflessly, sustaining life with quiet humility. It takes nothing and yet offers everything. Truly, breath, you take my breath away!

I also discovered that the rhythm of breath is deeply linked to our thought process. The rhythm of our breath influences the nature of our thoughts and the state of our mind, and the reverse is also true. During moments of anxiety, our breath quickens and becomes shallow. On the other hand, long and deep breaths calm the mind, making us more peaceful. These observations have led many before me to use breath as a tool to understand the mind and build a harmonious relationship with it. By consciously altering the way we breathe, we can influence our thought patterns and regain calm and clarity.

This idea resonates deeply with ancient wisdom. In Indian mythology, the Ramayana tells of Hanuman, the son of Vayu (the wind god), who helps Lord Ram—a symbol of virtue and righteousness to rescue Sita, his *Shakti* (power), from Ravana, the embodiment of evil and vice. To me, this story symbolizes how our breath, the son of Vayu, empowers the good within us to triumph over the evil of negativity. Awareness of breath calms the mind, sharpens our intellect and enhances our ability to discern right from wrong, helping us make better choices.

Through the practice of mindful breathing, I have come to appreciate air as a divine presence and life-sustaining blessing. Its humility in being invisible despite its omnipresence, tells us that the most essential forces in life often go unnoticed and are taken for granted. This realization made me reflect on how often we overlook this precious element. While each breath we take is a gift, billions today breathe polluted air. Our mindless actions leading to air pollution reflect a troubling disregard for the life force that breathes through all living beings. Recognizing air as a divine blessing compels us to protect its purity—not just for ourselves but for all forms of life and future generations. As a mark of respect and gratitude for this vital life force, I invite you to chant this mantra with every breath you take: *'Om Vayu Namah.'*

Om Akashaya Namah

(I Bow to the Element of Space)

"The void where all elements reside,

Where universes, planets and stars abide,

That infinite void,

In the absence of which all presence is devoid,

That element of nothingness holds substantial might,

Within which all Life plays in shades of dark and light.

To that element of Space, let me introduce thee,

That which embodies both Zero and Infinity!"

The classroom echoed with applause as Avinash recited these lines to his students. A mathematics teacher in the local high school, Avinash had just composed the impromptu verse to illustrate the concept of infinity. Inspired by the vastness of space, he felt it was the perfect metaphor to explain something so elusive and profound.

After the applause subsided, he turned to his class with a question.

"How do we represent infinity?" he asked, scanning their faces. "Infinity isn't a number, as any number can be defined. It isn't a quantity, as any quantity can be measured. So, how do we understand it?"

He let the silence linger for a moment before continuing, "Infinity is what we encounter when our ability to measure is exhausted. Many think of it as a very large number, or the opposite of zero—but it is neither. Infinity, by definition, is endless. And here's the paradox: only an entity without a beginning can never truly have an end. To understand infinity, you must first understand zero. And to understand zero, you must understand the element of space."

Avinash paced the front of the room as he elaborated. "Zero is like space—it has no beginning, no end, yet it holds a void within itself. This void accommodates everything: all elements, their combinations, and their infinite manifestations. Without this void, existence itself would be impossible. Zero, therefore, holds the key to all numbers. It is the starting point, the origin, and the also the key to the growth of numbers. As numbers grow larger, they rely on zeroes to grow—just as life when it grows, needs space to expand."

He paused, then asked, "But can anyone tell me what accommodates space?"

The class hesitated until a student, Rajul, raised his hand. "Nothing accommodates space. It simply exists," he said.

"Exactly!" Avinash said, his face lighting up. "Just as nothing accommodates space, zero has no beginning, yet it is where all numbers begin and eventually perish in it. No matter how large a number becomes, its negative counterpart will always reduce it to zero. Zero has no such negative counterpart and being transparent, it always reflects the positive and negative values added to it in their truest form. Infinity is not the opposite of zero or separate from it—it is in fact, a zero twisted upon itself, which is why we represent it as a loop."

Avinash moved to the chalkboard and drew a symbol for infinity. "And if you view in life, all entities are made of the five basic elements – Earth, Water, Fire, Air and Space. Of these five, the last element, Space is the one that embodies the concept of infinity. All other elements are finite; they originate and perish within this infinite fifth element. It is the vast, infinite stage where all existence—positive and negative—unfolds. Space is not the opposite of value; it is the container that holds all possible values. So you see, Zero is not the opposite of infinity, it is infinity itself."

"Sir," a student raised his hand. "What would be the value of space without the things it holds? Isn't it the things inside a space that make it valuable?"

"Indeed!" Avinash smiled. "The finite adds value to the infinite. But without space, where would you place the things you value? So isn't space, the container, ultimately more valuable? It's the coexistence of value and void—of space and elements—that makes up the cosmos. In Sanskrit, we call this element of space the *Akash Tattva*, and the void within it is referred to as *Shunya*—a term we also use for zero. The entire Universe exists in it, and I bow in reverence to it with the mantra:

"Om Shunyaya Namah,

Om Akashaya Namah."

The classroom was silent for a moment as the students reflected on the profound ideas their teacher had shared. Then, one by one, they began to clap again—this time, not for the poetry, but for the deeper understanding they had gained that day.

The Way Up

Long, long ago, from the vast emptiness of Space, the elements emerged. Air, Fire, Water, and Earth came alive to make the universe. Fire, unlike the others, instinctively aspired to reach high, its flames aiming for the skies, kept rising in an unrelenting quest for elevation. Earth and Water, inspired by Fire's upward movement, looked to it for guidance. To them Fire said, "Join me and I can try to uplift you as I rise."

Air, however, arrogant and proud of its higher status, laughed at Fire's efforts.

"Do you really think you'll be able to make it?" Air teased Fire.

"Being in an elevated state, you should be inspiring me instead." Fire replied.

Fire's words stirred Air with a streak of guilt, and reluctantly it joined Earth and Water as they entered Fire to seek the way up. Together, the elements started their upward journey as one team.

However, they soon began to feel their identities fading. Earth's solidity crumbled into ash, Water's flow evaporated into steam, and Air's freedom and purity dissipated into smoke. Alarmed by their imminent loss of self, each element reacted in desperation. Air expanded, taking on a gusty, windy form to save itself and blow out Fire. Earth hardened, growing dense and immovable. Water became vivacious, surging and swirling to douse the flames. Fire, overwhelmed by their resistance, began to dwindle.

Chaos ensued as the elements struggled against one another, each clinging to their individuality. Desperate for resolution, Fire turned to Space for guidance.

"Great Space," Fire called out, "I truly wish to help my friends ascend, but we are caught in a struggle over our identities. None of us can move forward."

Space, vast and serene, responded, "To uplift others, you must raise yourself first. Focus your energy, find your center and elevate yourself. Set an example, only then the others will follow."

Hearing this, Fire paused and meditated. It turned inwards, concentrating on a single point at its core, drawing its energy inward with unwavering focus. Rolling itself into a perfect sphere, Fire awakened to its essence with newfound gravity and strength. Rising higher and higher, it levitated beyond the Earth's gravity, and transformed into the self-gravitated Sun, sitting meditatively in the heavens, radiating light and warmth.

Below, the Earth, Water, and Air gazed up at the Sun that had now become a beacon of inspiration. Drawn towards its serene radiance, each of them found their way to rise. Earth took the form of tall trees and majestic mountains, seeking its light. Water ascended into clouds, embarking on a heavenly journey across the skies. Even Air, now humbled, looked up, realizing there was a place higher than itself. It rose higher into the ethereal realms uniting with Space to realize its infinite potential.

Ever since that day, this planet has orbited the Sun, looking up to it as a guide. And the Sun, in turn, inspires all elements on the planet to rise towards its light, radiating the timeless truth that one must raise oneself first to uplift the world around.

The Path and the Traveller

Richa had wandered far and wide, crossing continents and oceans in a career that took her to breathtaking places. She had stood atop snowy peaks, felt the salt spray of distant seas, and walked streets alive with the hum of unfamiliar languages. Her social media brimmed with snapshots of sunsets, bustling markets, and exotic plates of food. Four thousand two hundred and eighty followers liked, commented, and shared her adventures.

Yet beneath the applause and the dazzling pictures, Richa often felt an unspoken loneliness. She felt a hollow within herself that no number of travel experiences and social media likes seemed to fulfill.

In all her travels, the only constant companion she had was the Path. It stretched before her, sometimes winding through golden meadows, sometimes disappearing into misty woods. The Path was silent yet always there to lead her forward.

She often thought of the Path as a living being—her one true friend. It guided her when the skies were bright, supported her when the storms rolled in, and patiently waited when she paused to rest by a pool or stream. Yet, when she looked into the still waters to catch her reflection, she never saw the Path beside her. Its absence in the reflection made her uneasy and she would start walking again.

The Path, though invisible in the mirror, spoke to her through the crunch of gravel, the rustle of leaves and the soft thud of her shoes against the earth. It was the quiet voice that urged her onward, promising more wonders around the world.

One day, after years of wandering, Richa finally returned home. She stood at the doorstep of her small house that appeared weathered and warm, and looked back at the Path that had brought her there. A strange thought occurred to her, and she turned to it with a question.

"Will you come inside with me?" she asked the Path.

The Path seemed to smile, though it remained still. "It is not in my nature to enter homes," it replied. "I leave you here, at the threshold of rest and comfort. But I will wait for you, just beyond this door, ready to lead you whenever you wish to journey again."

Richa thoughtfully inquired, "Don't you want to see where I live? To meet the people I call my own?"

The Path replied, "I have seen you, Richa. I know your heart, your dreams and your fears. Through your eyes, I have glimpsed the world you carry within you. That is enough for me to know the home you've built and the ones you share it with."

She hesitated, unsure of how to respond. The Path continued, "We paths are wanderers, forever homeless yet always at home with the outdoors beneath the open sky. I exist for those who wish to journey, to learn and to grow. For the time we travel together, we are inseparable. The Traveller and the Path become one, we shape each other. But when you stop, I must step back, for it is in the nature of paths to wait until the traveler is ready."

"Hmm, and what if I don't ever come back to you." Richa asked after a deep thought.

"I am sure you will come, and even if you don't, I want you to know that I am not truly separate from you. I emerged from your mind and with your experiences I shall live within you in your memories forever. When you sit quietly, you will feel me there, as a part of your being. The Traveller and the Travelled are one within you. Through the path within, you can choose to travel the world outside you or explore the world within you."

Richa smiled at the Path, turned the key, and stepped inside. The warmth of the familiar space enveloped her as she sank into her chair.

The Path's words echoed through her mind as she sipped her coffee, *"Through the path within, you can choose to travel the world outside you or explore the world within you."*

Setting her cup aside, Richa closed her eyes and turned inwards. In the stillness, she felt the familiar presence of the Path, radiantly glowing and inviting her to explore the world within. With a quiet smile upon her lips, Richa followed the Path into the quiet corridors of her heart, finding a peace that quenched the hollow within her.

The Path outside waited patiently for her return, as Richa continued to explore the world inside to reach her soul's home within.

True Self

At the yoga retreat, *yogacharya* Arjun had posed some profound and interesting questions. He asked, "Who are you? What is identity? Is it merely a label or a passport that we carry to come into this world? What happens to it when life ends? Does death strip away our identity or is it the fading of identity that brings death? Or is identity something eternal, untouched by the loss of name and form?"

Pausing for a moment, he let the questions sink in. "Most of us fear death because we think it's the end of our identity. But is that fear rooted in truth or in a false understanding of who we really are?"

The room fell silent, with each of us pondering deeply on his questions. He wasn't seeking any answers. He only wanted us to reflect and understand the truth.

Carrying the questions in my mind I returned to my room. Sitting in my chair I reflected on them again. The questions stirred my thoughts and a story started taking shape in my mind.

I picked up my diary to write down the story:

* * * * * * * * * * * * * * *

Long ago, before time began, the Creator had only one element to start the creation with. It was Space, the first element. Space was vast, peaceful and infinite, mirroring the Creator's own essence. For eons, Space existed in stillness until a ripple stirred within her, and from that ripple, Air was born—a restless, untamed child. There was darkness all around and Air lacked a sense of direction. So Air darted in every direction, unbound and chaotic, until sparks began to fly from her movements. These sparks grew brighter and brighter until they formed a new element: Light.

But Light's arrival unsettled Space. She had grown used to Darkness, her silent companion. She had come to believe that Darkness was her very identity. When Light began to spread, illuminating her being, Space resisted the change fiercely.

"Stop this, Air!" Space cried. "Be still. Your movements bring Light, and Light will destroy me!"

Free-spirited Air, laughed. "Destroy you? I'm only bringing in Light and she's revealing what you truly are!"

The battle between Light and Darkness raged. Light was gradually consuming Darkness that kept shrinking further and further until only a sliver remained. With Darkness gradually being swallowed by light, Space felt insecure, she felt her end was near.

"Who am I without Darkness?" she cried.

Light, now fully grown approached her gently and said, "You are not what you think you are, you are not Darkness. Darkness was just an absence of Light. You are vast and eternal, far beyond my presence and absence."

At last, the final shadow dissolved, and Space braced for the end. But instead of vanishing, she found herself alive and fully illuminated. In that moment, Space realized that Darkness had never been her true identity. It had only been a veil, hiding her true nature.

"Now I see," Space said, in a voice filled with wonder. "I am neither Darkness nor Light. I am simply myself."

Air too was overwhelmed with the enlightenment that Light brought. All directions were visible now. Awestruck, Air realized the immensity of Space. Earlier, in the darkness, even a faint spark of Light would drive Air to move frantically towards it. But now, in full illumination, where all directions were clear, Air stood still. It felt calm and content, as if auto-tamed by the clarity that Light had brought.

Once resistant, Space now felt gratitude for Light. "You've liberated me from the false sense of identity and shown me who I truly am."

Light smiled. "I only revealed what was already within you."

****

As I finished writing, I reflected on how closely the story of Space reflects the story of each one of us. How often do we cling to false identities—names, forms and roles—believing they define us? These roles and labels become the masks we wear, hiding the vastness of who we truly are. And how often do we resist change, fearing it will destroy us, only to realize that the transformation reveals the unchanged, eternal self beneath it?

The next day, I shared the story with Yogacharya Arjun. He listened patiently and smiled as I finished. "Beautiful," he said. "You've captured the essence of the questions. Our true self isn't bound by the identities we create—it is eternal, holding all the identities within itself like Space holds light and darkness."

As I walked back, I found myself pondering the things I had allowed to define my identity—expectations, roles and fears. And I felt it is so important and liberating to ask ourselves: Who am I?

It can be the spark of light to illuminate the vast Space of our true self.

Life and Death

A Journey from Limited Self to Infinite Self

There was once a beautiful tree laden with ripe fruits. It was content with its existence in the sunshine, savouring the aroma of its flowers and fruits. One day as the wind blew; some ripe fruits fell to the ground. A passerby picked up a fallen fruit, relished it and thoughtlessly threw the seed onto the soil.

Once safely nestled inside the fruit, the seed now lay exposed and vulnerable. It felt abandoned, gazing helplessly toward the majestic tree it had come from. The parent tree, though caring at heart, did not heed its gazes asking for help. Deep in its wisdom, the tree knew this was the seed's path—a journey it had to undertake alone to realize its potential.

Dejected by the indifference of its own parent the seed began to mourn its fate. Just then, a young boy approached, picked it up, and gently buried it in the soil. This only added to the woes of the seed. Separated from light, air and warmth, the seed despaired, convinced it was buried alive. It felt it was in some deep dungeon, where getting help was impossible — even if it cried, no one would hear it. Surrounded by darkness, it saw no hope or possibility of survival. Unaware of its own potential the seed resigned to its fate, feeling almost dead.

Days passed and beneath the weight of the soil, as it struggled to breathe, it saw a tiny spark of hope – its inner strength. It became aware that the only help here could come from within. It decided to build on this strength and refused to give up.

It pushed against the heavy earth, instinctively fighting for survival. In its struggle, the seed's outer shell cracked and fell away. Though unsure if this was progress or loss, it noticed that the absence of the shell made movement easier. So it pushed harder.

A few days later it became aware of hair-like growth emerging from its downward pushes. It had managed to grow its first roots! These reached deep down into the soil and for the first time the seed tasted water.

Soon its body split into two fleshy wings. It wondered if it was getting ready for flight. It was amazed at the changes in its own body, and marveled at the process of trying to live by pushing hard. Despite the struggles, it was happy that it was still alive! In a place away from the world, with no one around to help, it had managed to survive and even grow! It now directly tasted the soil, about which it had only heard of from its parent tree. Indeed the soil and the water that the soil held, tasted like nectar, because this was 'hard-earned' food.

 Slowly feeding on and pushing hard, it grew a tiny shoot that stretched toward the surface, softening the soil with secretions as it inched closer to light.

One glorious morning it woke up and was dazzled by the light it saw. Yes, it was the sun! It had finally managed its way above soil!

Having found its way out of the soil, the little seed, now a tiny sapling, danced with joy and smiled. It looked at the sky above and the soil below, appreciating both as its nurturers. Taking a deep breath of fresh air, it felt alive in a way as never before. It spread out its arms to embrace the freedom of air and the sun's light.

As the sapling grew it became aware of its inner strength and potential. As a seed, it had seen grown up trees, but now through its own journey it had consciously witnessed the process of growth. *It realised that growth meant a constant effort and trust in one's ability to rise while going deeper to stay rooted.*

Its initial growth acted as a catalyst to boost and encourage further growth. As it grew further into a young plant, it saw many flowering plants around it and dreamed of bearing its own blossoms. It deepened its roots, drawing nourishment, to grow stronger and more beautiful. This phase was marked by tough competition, as every plant around vied for the best nutrients and sunshine. Each one was trying to be their best.

The competition that had started with enthusiasm gradually left the young plant drained and disheartened. It realized that true growth lay in focusing inward, not outward. So it stopped comparing itself with others and simply worked on what seemed to be best for itself.

With time, the young plant became a tall tree. Beautiful fragrant flowers adorned it and their intoxicating aroma filled the air. Passersby admired its beauty, and the tree basked in their praise with pride and joy.

Its ambitions soared once again when it saw a group children gather around a neighbouring tree. Human attention was too tempting to be forgone. It was now living on a plane where it felt that besides physical food, there was something more that it needed to survive; perhaps, mental food, or food for its ambitions! It wondered what the neighbouring tree had in special to attract children. "Oh it's the fruits!" it exclaimed, spotting the fruits hidden in the foliage of the neighbouring tree. A new desire took birth in its heart - the longing to bear fruit.

Bearing fruit required tremendous effort. The tree deepened its roots further, strengthened its branches to support the upcoming fruits, and worked tirelessly to draw nourishment from the earth. It was a tough exercise requiring it to work more hours than usual and resting only a little. This was much more demanding than producing flowers. The process was arduous, yet the tree pressed on, driven by the vision of its fruits. In the zest to make its dream come true, work didn't feel like work but a joyful activity. Despite the workload the tree didn't feel tired. It was beginning to realize that work itself doesn't exhaust us; rather, it is working against our own will that makes us feel weary.

Finally one day, when the first fruit appeared upon its branch, the tree rejoiced. In its joy it spread out its branches laden with fruits. Attracted by the sight, people gathered beneath its shade, to savour the tree's offerings. The tree stood tall and proud, feeling fulfilled.

But fulfillment came at a cost. Children climbed its branches, breaking some in their excitement. Others threw stones to bring down the fruit, bruising the tree's bark. The tree bore the pain silently, knowing it was part of its purpose. It was no longer just a tree; it had become a source of nourishment, joy and life for others. It felt happy about choosing a path of serving others.

One day, the tree watched as a child ate its fruit and discarded the seed onto the soil nearby. Memories flooded back and it recalled its own journey of struggle and growth from a seed. In that moment, the tree understood the indifference of its parent tree long ago. It had not been abandonment, but a silent acknowledgment of the wisdom that every seed must find its own way.

Reflecting on its life, the tree realized that its journey had been far more than a cycle of desires and fulfillment. It had been a process of self-discovery, transformation, and creation. As a seed, it had carried within it the blueprint of an entire tree and the potential to nurture countless others.

Looking up at the sky, the tree felt a profound connection to the infinite. It had stood rooted in one place all its life, yet it had come a long way - travelling through growth, ambition, hardship and joy. It had lifted the soil into the air, carried sunlight into its fruits, and touched the lives of countless beings.

It was not merely a journey from soil to fruits, but from the limited self to an infinite self...a journey that brought it closer to its true self. And all this came with the promise of hope that even if you lose yourself in creating a fruitful world, you're bound to create yourself and many others too in the process.

Twin Sisters – Life and Death

The universe began with the birth of two twin sisters; Life and Death. They were like two sides of the same coin, bound together yet destined for vastly different paths. Life was bubbling with energy and action, full of curiosity, vibrant, and eager to explore and create. Death, in contrast was more of an introvert, quiet, introspective, calm and wise.

As the universe unfolded, the sisters made their choices. Death chose to stay at the place of their origin, the still center of the circle of the universe, while Life ventured outward, traveling along its radius to explore its unknown circumference.

Life; like light, ventured into the dark unknown universe, illuminating every part of it, along her way. Like a thirsty explorer, she went all around to see the world from different angles and perspectives, gathering myriad views. On this journey, she left behind everything, yes, everything including Death.

She was silent like an empty vessel; when she began her journey. But as she gathered experiences —drops of joy, sorrow, discovery and loss—that filled her, her once quiet journey started resonating with the symphony of creation. Life could not help but create as she moved. From nothing, she brought forth everything: hunger and its satisfaction, questions and their answers, emptiness and its fulfillment.

All this while, Death remained at the center, unmoved and, untempted by Life's calls to join her. "Come, sister!" Life would shout. "It's so much fun to create. Come, see what I made!" But Death only smiled gently, rooted in her meditative stance. She knew that movement and creation were not her natural calling; she was destined to wait, and in waiting everything would eventually come to her. And she waited with this trust while her sister roamed.

As Life journeyed further along the circle, she began to grow weary. Her once-thrilling adventure started to become a heavy burden, her vessel now full to the brim was overflowing with the weight of countless experiences. With each step, she grew quieter and more reflective. She realized she had seen the universe from every angle, explored every perspective, yet something was missing. In her heart, she longed for the one thing she had left behind: her sister. Her peaceful face often floated before her eyes.

Turning inward, Life began her return to the center. The path grew stiller with each step, as if the universe itself was holding its breath. When she reached the origin, Death greeted her with open arms and a serene smile on her lips.

"Welcome home, sister," Death whispered.

Exhausted from the journey, Life sank into Death's lap, finally resting peacefully after a long time. In the stillness, she saw her sister as she had never seen before. Death was not aloof, as she had once thought, but wise and patient, preparing for her return all along. She had created a vast and deep space, ready to hold the immensity of experience that Life had gathered. Life realized that Death's stillness was not emptiness but the key to renewal, a womb where all experiences were deposited and from which creation would one day emerge anew.

As the two sisters embraced, the circle of the universe dissolved, and only the origin, the point of their mutual beginning and end, remained. In that timeless moment, Life slept deeply, cradled in her sister's arms.

And as Death waited, she knew that one day Life would awaken, ready to set forth on another journey, carrying all that had been as a seed of all that could be.

Light and Darkness

When the Universe came into existence, the elements were indistinct, flowing seamlessly into one another in an amorphous formation. There were no boundaries, no clear divisions, a sense of oneness and harmony prevailed through it. Yet, as the Universe grew from infancy to infinity, each element felt the need to define itself and drew boundaries to carve their identities, separating themselves from the rest. These elements now existed as tiny universes within the large universe, often clashing with each other, having forgotten the unity that existed at the time of their origin.

In this ever-expanding cosmos, Darkness lay peacefully asleep. It was her domain, vast and unchallenged, until Light suddenly came into existence. Light's arrival stirred Darkness, her sleep was disturbed and she bristled at this unwelcome intrusion.

"Who dares disrupt my solitude?" she muttered in irritation. Seeing Light illuminate the space, she grew resentful. "This is my realm! Leave at once or I shall curse you never to find rest."

Light, baffled upon hearing this voice coming from nowhere, had no idea where to go. The face of Darkness wasn't visible to Light as her illumination had rendered Darkness invisible.

Thus Light was cursed to wander around. But Light, being an eternal optimist, always looked at the brighter side of things. She took the curse as an opportunity. Instead of despairing,

she was delighted at the idea of exploring the world. She went
traversing mountains, oceans, and the endless skies.
Wherever she went, she added color and warmth with her
brilliant and cheerful presence. Meanwhile, Darkness,
confined by her own bitterness, found herself in turmoil. She
could not rest, for her curse had backfired.

Exhausted and frustrated, Darkness sought God's
intervention. "I cannot bear it any longer," she cried in God's
court. "Light has made my existence unbearable! She chases
me relentlessly, invading every space I inhabit. There is no
peace, no refuge for me. If this continues, one of us must
cease to exist!"

God turned to Light and asked for her side of the story. Light,
calm and composed, replied, "I hear a voice calling for me to
leave, but I see no one. How can I chase someone I have never
seen? I travel where I am drawn, bringing brightness wherever
I go. If my presence is disturbing, I do not mean it to be so. I
only seek your guidance."

God listened patiently, then spoke with a smile, "You are both
integral to the balance of this Universe. One cannot exist
without the other. Your conflict is born not of rivalry, but out
of misunderstanding."

Turning to Darkness, God said, "You fear Light because you
see her as your end. But the absence of one is simply the
presence of the other. You are two sides of the same coin,
bound together in an eternal cycle."

Then, addressing them both, God declared, "To ensure harmony, I decree that you shall share equal space and time. When Light reigns, Darkness will rest, and when Darkness falls, Light will take a break. You will coexist, not as adversaries, but as partners shaping the rhythm of existence."

God continued, "Each of you shall also manifest within the souls I created. Light, you shall symbolize virtue, self-awareness, and hope. And Darkness, you shall be the absence of these, symbolizing ignorance, doubt and fear. Light shall have the potential to undo the effects of ignorance, doubt and fear, by illuminating them and darkness shall soften the sharpness of Light's brightness and bring rest in weary times. Through your interplay, the Universe and the souls within it will evolve towards greater harmony. But when a soul is liberated from your duality, both of you shall dissolve and merge into me again."

Light and Darkness accepted this decree, and from that moment on, they ceased their quarrel. By day, Light illuminated the world, and by night, Darkness cloaked it in rest. To this day, together, they weave the eternal cycle of existence, each dissolving into the other as a reminder of their primordial unity.

And so, Light painted dawns and dusks with her brilliance, while Darkness embraced the stars, weaving silence into the night. Through their unity, the Universe continues to evolve from shades of darkness into colours of light—and back again—until the day both would merge into the infinite, where all boundaries would fade.

The saga continues...

Quest for Survival

We were tiny bacteria, thriving in the warm country of a petri dish, nourished by a smooth culture medium. Our culture was helping us grow, and we grew rapidly in booming colonies flourishing in abundance until we realized that our culture medium was over populated. The competition for space and medium was growing stiff with each passing moment. Some of us started secreting inhibitors to control the population growth, but there were others who continued reproducing recklessly. Chaos loomed, and survival seemed increasingly uncertain.

In the face of dwindling resources, a few of us made a daring decision. My friends and I resolved to explore beyond the confines of the petri dish, searching for a new medium, a new country, a new home where we could continue to thrive. It wasn't just about growth anymore; it was a matter of survival.

Once outside the petri dish, we encountered a vast, unfamiliar world teeming with life. We came across countless other strains of bacteria, strikingly similar to us yet with distinct food habits and survival needs. For the first time, I began to understand life beyond the boundaries of my country and culture. Though we could endure hunger for a few days, our quest for survival and a hospitable environment had only just begun.

Eventually, we found our way into a human host. We were excited at spotting a new medium ripe with potential. But our arrival was met with hostility. The temperature around us began to rise, an unwelcoming fever intended to drive us out. Yet, having struggled so much to reach this point, we hung on and endured the heat. This resilience strengthened our resolve to stay and we grew more confident of our survival inside the host's body.

Our triumph, however, was short-lived. The host launched a chemical attack. Antibiotics flooded the bloodstream, decimating my companions. For three days, I watched as one by one, my friends succumbed. By the end, I was left alone, weakened but alive, drifting through the host's bloodstream. The host's white blood cells patrolled relentlessly, hunting for intruders like me. Fear gripped me as survival now seemed impossible.

"Life in the dead medium of the petri dish had been so peaceful," I thought. "Here, in this living host, every moment is a battle." Yet, despite the fear and exhaustion, a small flicker of pride warmed me. I had survived so far. But my pride was short-lived, as I realized I had no escape. The host's defences were persistent, and I was cornered.

Desperate, I sought refuge in the subcutaneous alleys of the host, hiding from the white blood cell army while pondering my fate. I knew I needed to propagate my culture, to leave a mark. But before I could act, I felt my bacterial form weakening. My time as a bacterium was nearing its end. And then, something extraordinary happened.

In my final moments, I shed my bacterial identity and became part of the host. I was no longer an outsider; I was absorbed into something far greater than myself. The host's defences no longer perceived me as a threat. For the first time, I felt at peace.

The struggle to survive, to protect my smaller self, faded into insignificance. In becoming part of the host, I transcended my limited existence. No longer burdened by the fear of survival, I could think, grow, and contribute in ways I had never imagined.

I realized I wasn't my body; I wasn't my culture, but a spark of aliveness that survived beyond it all. Survival wasn't about clinging to an identity or defending it. It was about growing beyond it.

The realization filled me with awe. The fear I had carried for so long—the fear of the unknown, of losing myself—had blinded me to the truth. By letting go of my smaller identity, I had gained something far greater. I had become part of a bigger reality, where survival was no longer my concern. I was free to explore new possibilities, and grow as a part of this bigger organization. I felt like a drop that had become the ocean by merging in it.

And in that freedom, I found a new kind of life, a life not defined by individual struggles but by mutual growth based on unity. My journey as a bacterium had ended, but my evolution had only just begun.

The Diamond and the Coal

It was a wintry night, and the cold wind howled outside. Inside a cozy room, a heap of coal lay near the fireplace, ready to be burned for warmth. The lady of the house, seeking respite from the chill, removed her diamond ring and placed it on a stool near the fire. From the heap of coal, one piece looked up at the diamond and gasped in awe; "Ah! You look so beautiful! Just like a sparkling star," it exclaimed.

The diamond looked at the coal and gently smiled, "Thank you, but you and I are not so different. I was once like you, hidden beneath the earth's layers. For years I endured immense pressure, buried in darkness, until I hardened. It was much later that I realised my resilience was my strength. This brought clarity that reflected in my appearance and I began to transform, radiating with an inner glow. So I may appear different, but believe me, we are essentially the same."

The coal blinked in disbelief.

"You're kidding, aren't you? Look at me— dark and dusty. How could I ever become something as radiant and cherished as you? Are you telling me a true story or just some fantasy fiction?"

The diamond sighed. "It's true, my friend, but the beauty you see comes at a cost. And sometimes, I wonder if life as a coal might have been better than this."

This further surprised the coal. "Better? What's good about being a coal? We're just chunks of old wood, destined to feed this fire and turn to ash and smoke. But you're brilliant, cherished and valued. You'll live long after we're gone, perhaps even longer than the ones who possess you."

The diamond smiled wistfully. "My friend, you don't realise your worth. In burning you bring warmth and solace in the biting cold of winters. I appreciate how you sacrifice yourself to bring light and comfort to others. This kindness and warmth is true beauty. My beauty is only superficial; it sparks desire and breeds envy. The joy I bring to others is transitory - one that fades as quickly as it ignites. You, my friend, will burn brightly with purpose, leaving behind warmth and comfort. This is so liberating, while I will remain trapped in my form as a symbol of longing and unrest."

 "Trapped?" the coal asked thoughtfully, "Isn't your longevity a reward for what you endured?"

"Well, that's what it appears on the surface. But if you see from my perspective, this form has distanced me from my roots, setting me apart from all of you. Many of the coals that I grew up with don't even recognize me now. While you and many others like you aspire to have a form like mine, I wouldn't wish that kind of stress and pressure on anyone. I mean you don't need to pass through struggles to prove your worth. You don't need to become something else to be valued. Accepting who you are and knowing that you are beautiful and valuable in your own way, is no less a strength than endurance. Endurance alone is not a measure of one's strength or worth.

Come let's celebrate our oneness by embracing each other. Let fire melt the differences that separate us and liberate us in this moment."

The coal was silent for a moment, then said,

"Your words are full of wisdom - a wisdom that perhaps comes through your endurance. The more I am getting to know you, the more I am feeling inspired. Your form and brilliance are proof that transformation is possible.

You say there is no difference between us, but I see a world of difference! While we fear fire and the end it brings, you are fearless, ready to embrace us and the fire. You've conquered the fear of death, and that is truly inspiring. Our fear stems from ignorance, because we haven't seen what lies beyond our form. And perhaps we will die with this unfinished desire to be like you. We will die in want of transformation, while you; having attained the ultimate state, will attain true liberation as you are free from the fear of death. So do not devalue what you've become. Stay where you are. The world needs your light."

The diamond fell silent, deeply moved by the coal's perspective. As the fire crackled and consumed the coals, they glowed, radiating warmth and light into the room. Watching their glow fade into ash, the diamond reflected, *"In their sacrifice, they become a source of comfort. In my endurance, I reflect the light. Perhaps this is how we chose to define the purpose of our lives. Life isn't about how we appear or how long we live, but about the meaning we create and the goodness we leave behind."*

The Art of Dying

Evening had just set in. The sun dipping on the horizon, painted the sky with hues of crimson and gold. Shadows stretched lazily over the hills as a gentle breeze carried the scent of wildflowers. A Zen monk, walking along a winding path, paused to admire the beauty of the dying day when he noticed a man struggling to roll a large rock to the edge of a cliff.

Alarmed, the monk hurried over. "What are you doing?" he called out. "If that rock falls, it could hurt someone below!"

The man stopped and turned around. His face was pale and weary. "I wasn't thinking about that. I just wanted to test something," he muttered.

The monk frowned. "What could you possibly want to test by rolling a rock off a cliff?"

The man hesitated at first, and then with a wry smile said, "I was thinking of ending my life, but I'm scared. Falling from this height might only leave me broken, not dead. I thought poison might be easier, but these days, you can't trust anything, even poison might be adulterated. I don't want any more suffering—just an end. Do you know of a surer way to die painlessly and without risk?"

The monk was taken aback but remained calm. Concluding the man wasn't in the best of his senses; he placed a gentle hand on the man's shoulder and said, "Why would you want to die? Life is—"

"Painful!" the man interrupted, in a voice heavy with anguish. "My parents died a few months ago. My wife is quarrelsome and unfaithful. My children waste my hard-earned money. And as if that wasn't enough, I lost my job to my employer's incompetent relative. Every door I turn to is shut. There's nothing left for me." His voice cracked as he knelt before the monk, tears streaming down his face. "Please, just tell me how to die."

The monk, filled with compassion, helped the man to his feet. "Come with me," he said. "I know someone who can help you."

The monk led the man to his Master, a serene figure seated in a simple room inside the monastery. Bowing deeply, the monk said, "Revered Master, this man is here to learn the art of dying."

The Master looked at the man with calm, penetrating eyes. After a moment, he said, "It will take time to learn this art. I hope you are not in a hurry to die. Are you?"

The man, a bit confused by the master's question, but eager at the thought of finding an answer to his suffering, replied, "No, as long as it works and is painless, I'm willing to wait."

"Very well," said the Master. "Sit here, close your eyes, and remain still. Let whatever comes to your mind flow freely. Do not resist it."

The man sat and closed his eyes. At first, he was consumed by restless thoughts. Memories of his parents' deaths surfaced, followed by anger at his wife and worry for his children. His employer's betrayal replayed in his mind, and bitterness twisted within him. He clenched his fists and shifted uncomfortably, wondering if this strange method would work.

An hour passed, and his restlessness grew unbearable. He opened his eyes and said, "If I sit here doing nothing, who will look after my family?"

The Master smiled gently and said, "You were going to die, right? You must have thought about it before. So, the one who would have cared for them after you will take care of them now."

The man froze. The truth of the Master's words struck him, stirring his thoughts. He reminded himself of his misery and closed his eyes again, resolving to continue.

Another hour passed. His mind now questioned the technique itself. *'Will this really help me die? Isn't this just wasting time? At least falling off a cliff or taking poison would be quicker.'* Doubts swirled, in his mind and he opened his eyes.

Looking at the Master peacefully seated before him, he said, "I really doubt if I will die this way. Two hours have passed and nothing happened so far."

The Master gently replied, "You said you were not in a hurry. Still if you doubt my method, you can try something of your own."

The man recalled the harsh and risky techniques he had tried earlier and decided to stay. He sat again with his eyes closed.

Days turned into weeks. Gradually, the storm in his mind began to subside. The thoughts of his misery started to fade away from his mind like ripples fading on a still pond. He felt at peace. The restlessness of his mind ceased and it seemed as if a burden had lifted off his heart.

Meanwhile, his disappearance had made his family anxious. They struggled to get their lives back to normal in his absence. With no one to depend on, his children were forced to find work. His wife, now alone, began to realize the value of his presence. They grew more disciplined and self-reliant. Even his former employer, dissatisfied with the relative who had replaced him, longed for the man's return.

Three months passed. One day, the Master said, "Open your eyes."

The man hesitated. For the first time, he didn't want to open his eyes. He felt no need to return to the world he had left behind.

"You are dead already," the Master said. "You may go now."

The man opened his eyes slowly. As he looked around, the world seemed different. It felt brighter and lighter. Although everything was the same as before, it felt anew as if he had opened his eyes in the true sense for the first time.

He bowed deeply to the Master and said, "I understand now. The end I sought was not of the body but of the chaos within me. Physical death wouldn't have liberated me from the tribulations of my mind. In sitting here, I didn't gain anything, but I lost all my negativity, my anger, despair, and my attachments. Though my body remains, I've died a truer death and feel reborn into peace. I have learned the art of dying."

The Master smiled. "Now go, and live."

Body and Beyond

Born as a tiny ripple upon the vast surface of the ocean, I gradually grew up to be a fun-loving wave. I played with waves and tides, rolled with the winds and sparkled under the golden touch of the Sun. Life was simple—rise, fall, merge and rise again.

While playing upon the ocean with other waves - grandma wave would often point out to the high tides and say, "Look at them, they're so graceful and tall. They're the pride of the ocean." And I would awe at the splashes they made. Inspired, I looked up, hoping to soar like them one day and kept practicing, gathering momentum.

As waves we trained to glide, jump, roll, splash and twist. We usually trained at night, as the Moon was considered to boost our energies and uplift us. But we were forbidden to look at the Sun directly as he was notorious for hypnotizing the waves.

One day in the faint light of dawn I saw waves ahead of me crashing against the shore. I was stunned by what I saw. We were surrounded by the shore on all sides and if by any chance any of us were to fall out over to the shore, death was certain! It made me ponder on the inevitability of death.

Just then the view of the rising Sun pulled me out of my reverie. Initially by instinct I was turning my back to avoid looking at him directly. But then, I paused and thought if death is inevitable then why not get a glimpse of the Sun before I finally pass away. I turned around and what I saw changed me forever. I saw the Sun cresting the horizon, dressed in brilliant orange. He looked magically pristine and captivating. His brilliance was hypnotic, and his pull irresistible.

"Are you the Sun?" I called out amazed.

The Sun smiled and said, "Yes, I am. Would you like to come with me to explore a freedom beyond the tides?"

I smiled back and shyly returned, without saying anything. I kept reminding myself of the community's laws to avoid him. But even as I turned back I found it hard to forget his smiling face. He had surely hypnotised me. A longing stirred within me and I found myself yearning to reach that luminous orb beyond the sky.

The Sun's radiant face crossed my thoughts every now and then and I felt the strong need to look up to him. The kicking around on the Ocean waters and having fun with my siblings no longer attracted me.

From that day, each morning I waited for the Sun to arrive and silently stole glances at his lovely face. One day the Sun saw me looking at him, and I blushed.

He extended his hand – a luminous ray. I held on to it and ascended. I rose into the unknown dreaming of the sun's warm embrace as I left behind my oceanic playground and friends. My friends cried as they saw me leaving. "Oh don't go, you'll lose all that you have! Please don't go," they pleaded.

But despite their pleas, I left, as if destined for a celestial journey. I looked down at them, they were crying, "Oh she is no more!" I felt sorry for them, and wanted to let them know that I was still alive. But soon I realised I had indeed lost my form. It was obvious now why my friends couldn't see me. My body was no longer the fluid wave it had been. Yet, I felt I was still able to flow. Perhaps fluidity wasn't a material thing. It was my innate nature that I carried with me beyond my body. Weightless, I drifted, ascending higher and higher. Riding the winds, racing through the sky, I felt untethered, infinite. Had I attained the freedom the Sun promised?

As I got closer to the Sun, I felt the fiery heat coming from him. It jolted me to a sudden awakening from my blind attraction towards him. Having lost my physical body, I was doubtful if embracing the Sun would make me lose my spirit as well. Wanting to hold on to my essence and my fluidity, I stepped back.

 The Sun laughed, seeing me retreat. "Come on, why are you scared? Merge your essence in me and you'd rule the skies," he said. But I wasn't ready to surrender my freedom and soul, not even for the kingdom of the skies in return. My soul was the only thing I could now call my own, so I held on to it.

In that moment I felt content with my spirit, with my own being that I had never ever closely observed and admired enough. The loss of the liquid body had made me much lighter and more fluid than my earlier form. Though the view from above was amazing; when I looked down at the ocean, memories flooded my mind and my heart longed to go back home. Here in the sky, I stood as a total stranger, missing my friends and family. I decided to find a way back home. But first I needed to move to a cooler region, to have some respite from the Sun's heat.

I started moving towards the hills. There I met cold waves of air. They reminded me of the ocean waves; resembling them just a little ethereal and ruffled up. For a moment I felt I was home.

They flowed like water waves, but did not compete with each other for individual excellence like the ocean waves. They were more at ease and worked towards common goals in unison.

They moved to colder places to settle as icicles and to warmer places when they wished to glide around. Some of them simply played around with the branches of trees while others loved to blow near the ocean and tickle the water waves. I was viewing life from a totally different perspective and loved my role as an air wave. I could now travel long distances at greater speed in lesser time!

At times I would grow nostalgic and visit the ocean to meet my friends. But even as I could see them playing they seemed unaware of my invisible presence. I realised that I needed a liquid body to communicate with them - to share with them all my experiences out of the body.

So I moved up towards the glaciers where I saw frozen snowflakes queued to pass the heating test. I settled as a snowflake and waited for my turn in the queue. The molten snow-flakes closest in appearance to water would pass over to serve the vast plains before entering the ocean again. Though I had known what it meant to be like water, I realized knowledge alone was not enough; one had to 'become' water to pass this test.

It was a long process. My body was stiff; I could hardly move an inch. Frozen, I shut my eyes and waited patiently until I had gathered enough warmth to turn into water again. I'm not sure how long I was in that meditative state but the funny thing was; when I just got comfortable in one state, it was time to move to another state!

Fluid and agile once more, I found myself floating on a river, falling speedily through mountains. I wanted to rush back to the ocean as soon as possible but the way was long and I decided to enjoy the journey rather than worry about my destination.

Flowing through gigantic boulders, surrounded by lush forests, gliding down the waterfall I had the most exhilarating ride of my life! By the time I reached the plains I was exhausted, but as a part of a river I had yet to serve the plains before I could finally reach home and rest.

It was an eventful journey through the plains. The banks on either side of my river flourished with green fields and tall trees. I felt happy and proud to have contributed to their growth. Some of my co-travelers perished on the way. But I knew they were alive in some other form, maybe as a tree, grass or a plant. Having experienced life beyond the body, I was sure, that we stay alive even if the body is shed. Not everyone who started from the glacial heights made it to the ocean, some perished, some lost track and some decided to settle in the plains.

I had made new friends on my way and wanted them to meet my old friends from the ocean. I was imagining a grand reunion. One fine morning, I saw we were close to the ocean. I was finally returning home in my original liquid body. I was excited and hoped to meet my family and friends and tell them that I had made it back through the arduous journey.

It was the first time I saw the shore closely enough and touched it without crashing dead on it. While I had been inside the ocean, going out of it had meant death to me. I had associated the shore with death since then. This was the first time I was traversing the shore to go into the ocean from outside; perhaps this made all the difference! *The shore instead of being the gate to death became my gate to life- a passage to return home.*

Then I looked at the ocean as I had never seen it before. Everything was the same, but seemed so different. I saw the ocean as one huge being, who breathed waves in and out. We as waves had constantly been rising and falling, thinking it was we who went high or low. We had constantly been taking up new forms in the same body without ever realising it. We had been attributing all the credits and discredits of our rise and fall to our own efforts. But reality incorporated a much bigger scene than we as waves in the Ocean could ever imagine. We had always seen ourselves as waves, but that day I saw we were the Ocean!

I was perhaps too late to return. My whole family had perished. To my disappointment my old grandma, my parents and my siblings, no one was there. The whole place was now inhabited by the third generation descendants of my siblings; they greeted me but never recognised me. I was happy to be home, but sad at my loss. Even though I knew they were alive in some other form, yet I wished to see them again in the form that I had known. Overcome with grief I thought "Now, who shall I share my stories with? "

This momentary sadness was taken over by my expanded vision in which I saw all of them again in the water of the ocean, in the new waves, in the waves crashing upon the shore, and even in the invisible breeze. They were all around me.

Having experienced my own spirit in different bodies, I could visualize my entire family as one big spirit distributed into different bodies. A feeling of a much greater reunion took over me and I danced with joy. I jumped and splashed and soared high, crashing back without fear. It was the happiest feeling ever, a blissful joy springing from within. A feeling that I was home! Not in terms of a place, but I felt at home in the vast ocean of existence. As everything around me was surrounded by the ones I could call mine. No one seemed separate or apart, they were all a part of me. We were all one soul, one big family, the Universe!

Then I looked up at the Sun, and thought if I had known that we were the same spirit in different bodies, when I met him, I would have even stayed up there. But in the form of the Sun the spirit had a different role to play and it was placed appropriately in the entire sequence of events which seemed to fall perfectly in place now.

Later I took up the job of a wave trainer and encouraged my student waves to explore the areas near the shore and look at the Sun and rise with it. I wanted them to explore, feel uninhibited and experience their greater reality. There was nothing to fear now. With this I knew they too would discover that even if the body perishes, you continue to live on...

Values

The Banyan Tree

It was a hot summer afternoon. The roads, scorched by the sun, radiated heat and the sky stretched out harsh and unrelenting. Not a bird stirred from its shady nest. Even the breeze had abandoned its coolness, and the hot air seethed with the sun's wrath.

Sweat trickled down my back as I trudged along the blistering road, longing for respite. Then, in the distance, I spotted a Banyan tree and heaved a sigh of relief. Its presence felt like a refreshing oasis amidst the blazing heat. The promise of its shade quickened my weary steps and I headed towards it. Reaching it, I sank against its sturdy trunk and wiped the sweat off my forehead, feeling fortunate to have found such refuge.

Looking up, I saw birds resting upon its branches, peacefully perched in the shade of their 'Big Daddy'. A wave of gratitude flowed from my heart for the Banyan. In a commercialized world, this large-hearted tree freely offered shelter to birds and shade to weary travelers like me. At that moment, it seemed to me nothing less than a demigod.

Overwhelmed, I found myself speaking to it.

"How long have you been here?" I asked

A deep, ancient voice answered, "Ever since I emerged from Mother Earth's womb…" The Banyan paused, as if lost in deep thought. I remained silent, sensing he had more to say.

We sat in silence, for some time. The Banyan had not spoken in many years, and silence was not unusual for him. But I wasn't used to this kind of meditative silence yet. It made me all the more anxious and curiously I put forth another question "Why do you send down roots from your branches?" I asked hoping to know more about him.

 The Banyan grinned, "You know I just got a creative knack. I thought if roots could make branches, then branches could also make roots. I tried it, and—well, here I am!"

I smiled, enchanted by his playful wisdom. Forgetting the heat, I leaned in, eager to learn more.

"But why grow downward?" I pressed. "You had the potential to rise endlessly toward the sky. People always seek to move upward, to reach greater heights. Why did you choose a path that seems like regression?"

"Hmmm .... " A deep pause followed before the Banyan continued, "Do you want me to answer this or would you like to find out for yourself? I believe discoveries are fun!" he laughed.

I thought for a while, and said, "Indeed discoveries are fun, but this one, I'd like to hear from you."

The Banyan took a deep breath and said, "Like all trees, I was taught to grow toward the light. And so I did. My roots dug deep while my branches stretched high. I felt like a candle burning at both ends. I was as much below the ground as I was above it. Rising to the light and reaching for the sky seemed to be my ambition and purpose of life. The information in my genes guided me to go deeper for a greater stability, in order to rise higher. I was trying my best to achieve both. But as I climbed higher, something within me told me that I must reach a *respectable height*. But how high is this 'respectable height', was a big question.

I really did not know how high I should be going. Once out of the ground, I moved up with the momentum of reaching the sky. But the more I grew, the farther the sky seemed. No matter how high I reached, it only receded, always just beyond my grasp.

My self-set challenge 'to always be in the light' made me feel surrounded by the unknown. The farther I went away from my roots; the realms became more and more unfamiliar. The pursuit of light became a pursuit of the unknown. An endless quest where with every new height, I realized how much more there was to know.

That's when I looked back. The path I had travelled though covered in my own shade, felt known, familiar—a kind of light within darkness. But ahead, in the dazzling heights, was a sort of darkness within light—because I had no idea where it would lead.

That's when I understood: Light is knowledge, and darkness is ignorance.

It was then that I started growing downwards, towards the 'light' of the known. You see it as 'regression', but for me it's been progress all along. And the height where I hit this realization was the *respectable height* that I had been searching for. It was the moment I gained respect in my own eyes, for having discovered this new dimension of 'light'."

I sat in awe, absorbing his words. The Banyan had not only reached for the light—he had learned to become it. His growth was not just linear but all-encompassing, embracing both the sky above and the earth below in equal measure!

As I left his shade and stepped back into the sun, I looked back in reverence, carrying the light of his wisdom with me.

Desire and Renunciation

Desire, the son of a wealthy businessman, and Renunciation, the daughter of a minimalist Brahmin, were neighbours in their late teens. Desire had everything one could wish for—wealth, luxury, and a life of indulgence. A casanova at heart, he flaunted his red Ferrari, charmed the most attractive girls in town, and surrounded himself with friends who enjoyed his riches more than his company.

His most striking and constant companion was Problem. She was frequently seen by his side, appearing in new attire each time, as if she owned an infinite wardrobe. Desire's younger sister, Reputation, idolized Problem, pressuring their father to buy her new clothes every week to keep up. Though Desire and Reputation were the pride of their family, neither of them had a single friend they could trust beyond their wealth.

Desire was a pampered child and raised in a lavish lifestyle. He grew up to believe that money was the foundation of survival. The mere thought of losing it made him deeply insecure.

Renunciation, on the other hand, lived by the principles of simplicity. Her parents had taught her to embrace a life of minimalism, taking pride in being independent of luxury. She scorned those who flaunted wealth, believing them to be enslaved by materialism. Though kind to others, Renunciation was sort of unkind to herself, as she would often force herself into forgoing simple pleasures of life. She even denied herself small treats, like accepting a piece of cake offered by a friend, viewing such indulgences as unnecessary extravagance.

She despised Desire, and viewed him as a personification of everything she rejected. Desire, in turn, saw her as a self-righteous girl, needlessly proud of her plain existence. Yet, deep down, he was unsettled by her indifference. It baffled him—why was she the only girl in town who seemed utterly unimpressed by him?

Despite this tension, their fathers were good friends. Renunciation could not understand why her wise father, who had raised her on the ideals of simplicity, associated with a man whose family lived in excess. One evening, unable to contain her frustration, she confronted him.

"Father, why have you taught me to live with the bare minimum, yet you remain friends with those who live in extravagance?" she demanded.

Her father, seeing the turmoil in her eyes, responded gently, "Everyone chooses how they wish to live. I do not interfere with their choices."

"But shouldn't you at least guide them? If it's not in the best interest of humanity, don't they need to be taught, the way you taught me?" she insisted.

He smiled. "How am I to decide what is best for others? Each of us has an inner guiding principle that shapes our choices. Even when we preach, people interpret words in their own way. I have not imposed my views upon you—you have chosen to follow your interpretation of my teachings. Ask yourself, why do you choose what you choose?"

She fell silent stunned by the stark truth of his words.

Her father continued, "What is said or taught in words is always insufficient, it is the way we live our life that becomes our true teaching to the world. The guiding principle within us takes care of the universal good, and I trust it is a fool proof mechanism that maintains equilibrium in the universe. After all, the one who created such a vast and magnificent universe isn't a fool to design it without looking into possible errors and their remedies. There must be something inbuilt to set it right, even if it ever goes wrong".

Her father's words lingered in her mind. That night, she reflected on her beliefs and questioned herself, "Is my way of life truly superior, or is it simply another extreme?" She reviewed the merits of her simplicity—independence, adaptability, concern for the environment and a life free from clutter. Yet, she had denied herself the experience of life's simple joys.

In contrast, Desire's indulgent lifestyle seemed full of excitement, but she recognized its dangers—dependency, addiction, and the endless cycle of working to sustain extravagance. The two contrasting lifestyles felt poles apart and she wondered if there could be a middle path?

The next evening, as she walked in the garden, she noticed a cat chasing a mouse. It pounced, caught its prey, and devoured it. Satiated, the cat curled up, ignoring a larger rat scurrying nearby. It had no greed, no compulsion to hunt beyond its need.

A realization struck her. The cat followed no forced austerity, nor did it indulge unnecessarily. It simply followed an innate balance, taking only as much is required. Was this the equilibrium her father spoke of? The way the universe regulates itself?

This incident changed her and over time, Renunciation let go of her scorn and came to accept the reality of different lifestyles. When she saw Desire, she no longer felt the need to look away. One day, she even smiled at him. Desire, surprised yet pleased, welcomed this change. Gradually, they started talking, and an unlikely friendship blossomed.

Desire found in Renunciation something deeper than he had ever known, a companionship not based on wealth but on understanding. From her, he learned that happiness could be found in the simple things of life. He discovered that a moment of kindness was more fulfilling than a night of revelry, and a walk on dew-laden grass could bring more joy than the fleeting admiration of strangers.

As Desire spent more time with Renunciation, he found himself drawn away from Problem. Her influence over him

faded. Reputation, too, changed for the better, no longer
feeling the need to outshine others with material possessions.
Renunciation, in turn, realized that there was no harm in
enjoying simple pleasures like sharing a piece of cake, a
birthday celebration, or moments of laughter with friends. She
understood that celebrating occasions to bring joy to others
was not indulgence; it was kindness in another form.

Together, they learned that life wasn't about extremes. It was
about balance, about finding joy without attachment,
embracing simplicity without deprivation. And with the dawn
of this understanding, both of them found a freedom and
peace that they had never before known.

Aloneness and Loneliness

"Alone we all come and alone we all shall go"

He was out on a business tour. When he returned, he saw his home engulfed in flames. He screamed in anguish as he rushed forward, desperate to save his family. But a neighbour held him back, it was too late. The fire raged as fire-fighters struggled to control it. He watched helplessly as his world crumbled to ashes right before his eyes.

Overwhelmed by grief, he collapsed onto the street, sobbing. Neighbours surrounded him, offering words of comfort, but their voices faded into the void of his despair.

The Master knelt beside him, placing a gentle hand on his shoulder. The man clung to him as though grasping for something solid in his shattered world.

"I have lost everything, Master," he wept. "My wife, my children, my home—everything is gone. What am I to do now? What reason do I have to live now?"

The Master embraced him, allowing his sorrow to flow freely. He sat beside the grieving man in silence, offering neither words nor advice, but only his comforting presence. As time passed, the onlookers and neighbours, seeing there was little they could do, slowly dispersed, leaving him alone to watch the last embers fade into ashes.

Then, the Master gently said, "Come with me."

With nowhere else to go and nothing left to hold onto, the man followed. At the monastery, the Master offered him water and a quiet space to rest. No words could mend what was broken, so they sat together in silence, allowing grief to settle like dust after a storm.

The next morning, as sunlight filtered through the serene corridors, the Master gently guided him to sit in meditation — to steady his heart, ease his sorrow, and begin his journey anew.

At first, the man's grief surged even stronger. Each time he closed his eyes, the fire roared back to life in his mind. He sobbed, opened his eyes, shut them again, and wept until exhaustion took over. But little by little, between the waves of grief, there were moments of stillness.

Days passed, then weeks. The monastery became his refuge. When he felt ready, he asked the Master if he could stay until his home was rebuilt.

"Stay as long as you need," the Master replied.

Months later, he returned to his new house and resumed his life, but nothing felt the same. The meals tasted hollow. The silence at the dining table was unbearable. Though the world moved on, he remained tethered to the past.

Seeking comfort, he often visited the Master. One day, he asked, "Master, don't you feel lonely, living here all by yourself?"

The Master smiled. His eyes were calm and peaceful.

 "There is a difference between being alone and feeling lonely," he said. "Loneliness is a sadness that comes when you place your happiness in something outside yourself. But when happiness arises from within, you no longer need to seek it elsewhere."

"How do I find happiness within, when all I feel is emptiness?" the man asked.

"Embrace your aloneness. Feel the peace in it. In being alone, you meet yourself in solitude. As you become more aware of this peace, you will become more aware of your individual nature. It is something that connects you to everything. In this awareness, when you can feel your entire world within yourself, you will find that you are never truly alone."

The Master's words inspired the man to commit himself to meditation. Though the incident of the fire still haunted his dreams, he no longer recoiled from it. Slowly, his grief faded in the light of a deeper truth.

One day, the Master asked him, "Do you still miss your family?"

The man smiled with peace in his eyes, "I once believed that fire of the hearth united us; until another fire tore us apart.

But now, I see beyond union and separation; there's a oneness within, which no fire can destroy.

The Master smiled, "That's really good."

And the man smiled back, his eyes brimming with understanding. He was alone but not lonely any more.

Story of a Kingdom

*"A king is not one who is served by many; even the ever needy beggar of Want is served by the majority.
The true king does not require to be served by anyone; just like the ever peaceful Contentment"*

Want, the beggar, had been in a pitiable state when Contentment ruled the kingdom. Though a few kind-hearted souls showed him mercy and helped elevate his condition, he took advantage of their generosity and continued begging. Over time, Want transformed into a perpetual and wealthy beggar.

Eventually, Want conspired with his devious ally, Temptation, to overthrow Contentment. Together, they orchestrated a treacherous plot, exiling Contentment and taking control of the markets and towns. Under Want's tyrannical rule, the inhabitants of the kingdom became slaves to his insatiable demands.

Want's wives—Indulgence, Greed, and Lust—squandered the kingdom's resources, passing their reckless ways on to their sons: Anger, Chaos, and Laziness. Anger was a dangerous troublemaker who even threatened his parents. Chaos lived up to his name, embodying confusion and disorder, while Laziness, ever the sycophant, vowed to carry Want's destructive legacy to greater heights.

However, neither Want nor his family possessed the capability to manage the vast resources they had acquired. The kingdom descended into ruin, drawing the attention of a neighbouring ruler: Discipline.

Discipline, a stern and unyielding king, was determined to rid the Earth of Want and his incapable heirs. Though his own kingdom was well-organized and efficient, Discipline was infamous for his harsh policies and excessive taxation, which left his subjects burdened and discontent.

With persistent attacks, Discipline eventually overpowered Want, imprisoning him and his sons for life. The anarchy of Want's rule was over, but the people's happiness remained elusive. The crushing taxes imposed by Discipline made survival a constant struggle.

It was during this time of hardship that Love arrived in the kingdom, accompanied by his wife, Peace, and their daughter, Bliss. Love's warm and approachable nature endeared him to the people. He listened to their grievances, helped them in need, and quickly won their hearts.

One day, King Discipline caught sight of the radiant Bliss and was captivated by her beauty. However, his pride prevented him from marrying the daughter of a commoner, and he dismissed the idea. Yet, Bliss's image haunted him, and he wrestled with his feelings in silence.

Meanwhile, Love, aware of the people's suffering, approached Discipline to request a reduction in taxes. Impressed by Love's courage, Discipline agreed, but only on the condition that Bliss marry him.

Love, valuing his daughter's autonomy, replied, "The choice of a groom is hers alone. I cannot take that right from her." Furious, Discipline imprisoned Love and sent a message to Peace, declaring that Love would only be freed if Bliss agreed to marry him.

Bliss, seeking her father's freedom and the well-being of the people, consented to marry Discipline on the condition that he lower the taxes. Discipline agreed, releasing Love and reducing the burden on the kingdom's people.

Bliss's arrival marked a turning point in Discipline's life. While he initially intended to mold her into a traditional queen, Bliss's simplicity and grace softened him. Over time, she transformed him, teaching him the value of kindness and humility. Their union bore a son named Compassion.

When Compassion turned eighteen, he ascended the throne. Under his rule, the kingdom flourished, and the people's hearts were filled with joy. Compassion invited the exiled Contentment to return and serve as his chief advisor, ensuring wise and balanced governance.

Later, Compassion married Contentment's daughter, Wisdom. This further strengthened the kingdom's foundation. Together, they ruled with fairness and foresight, making the kingdom a realm of peace and prosperity.

The Balloon of Ego and the Stream of Breath

From the eternal union of Consciousness and Energy was born a beautiful and bright off-spring, full of potential. They named their child, Mind. Mind was a quiet observant child, but Mother Energy, a lively soul, wanted him to play around, have fun and explore the world around him. So she gave him two gifts: a Balloon of Ego and a Stream of Breath to bring it to life.

Mind observed that with every puff of Breath into the balloon of Ego, it would expand and start rolling about in the space around. Mind delighted in the game, chasing the balloon as it moved. This kept him occupied for a considerable time; the cheerful inflation of the Balloon brought him memorable moments of joy. Yet, inevitably, the Breath would seep out, leaving the Balloon deflated and still. Saddened, Mind would pause, but Mother Energy would gently coax him, "Blow into it again, my child, and keep it rolling."

And so the cycle continued—breathing life into the Balloon, chasing it, and mourning its stillness when it deflated. Through this game, Mind explored new corners of the vast Space, but his focus never strayed far from the Balloon.

One fateful day, the Balloon of Ego burst. Mind was left holding only the Stream of Breath, unsure what to do. Accustomed to exhaling for blowing up things, Mind blew the stream of breath into the infinite Space around, hoping to recreate the joy of inflation. Yet no matter how much or how forcefully he blew, the vast Space remained unyielding, impossible to fill. Confused, Mind thought, *"If a small balloon could expand, why not this great Space?"*

But he failed to see that when he played with the Balloon of the Ego, he stood outside it and was much larger than it. Now, surrounded by Space, he was but a tiny part of the whole and completely engulfed by it.

Consciousness, who had been observing the Mind all along, was quite amused at this and finally spoke. "Mind, my child, try turning the Breath inward, rather than outward."

Mind looked at him, a bit hesitant at first, but followed the advice. Slowly and steadily, he directed the Stream of Breath inward, breathing deeply into himself. Initially, nothing seemed to happen, but gradually, with patience, a quiet transformation began. Mind, who had always felt scattered in chasing the Ego, became more settled and calm. His awareness coalesced, and he took the shape of an awakened, breathing Being.

Having found clarity and consciousness within himself, Mind saw the vastness of Space in its true form. He understood that the Balloon of Ego, while playful and captivating, had always been merely a small fragment of a greater reality. He also realized the difference between breathing out and breathing in. Breathing out had kept him chasing the fleeting joys of the Ego, tethered to its inflation and deflation, making him lose self-awareness. Breathing in on the other hand, made him quieter and more aware of himself and his connection to the infinite reality around him.

From that day on, Mind practiced the ritual of breathing — creating a balance of incoming and outgoing breaths. He had discovered a rhythm within himself that needed no chasing. Breathing out to engage with the world and breathing in to anchor himself within. The cycles of happiness and sadness, tied to the Balloon of Ego, faded away and were replaced by a deeper harmony.

Grateful, Mind thanked Mother Energy for the gift of Breath and Father Consciousness for the wisdom to use it. Together, they smiled, watching Mind grow and evolve, with awareness in the boundless Space.

Contentment

Nestled in a quiet valley by the riverbank, lay Rocky; a small white stone, surrounded by other rocks. Close to it rested Granito, a larger, darker rock and Rocky's dearest friend. Granito, with its broad surface, made a comfortable seat, while Rocky, being smaller, was often kicked around by passersby.

"You're the fairest rock I've ever seen," Granito often said, admiring Rocky's smooth, spotless surface. Rocky, unaware that Granito hadn't seen many other rocks, and that the compliments stemmed from kindness, began to believe it was special. Pride swelled within it, causing it to forget their friendship and feel superior to Granito.

As days went by, Rocky grew proud and arrogant. When boys from the nearby village came to play, they would kick and toss the stones near the riverbank. Most stones enjoyed the rough and tumble, rolling about in joy. But Rocky hated it.

"Life on earth is good for nothing!" it complained. "We sit in the mud only to be kicked around by these little rascals for their amusement. Don't we have any self-respect? How can anyone just step on me while I'm napping and throw me around like I'm nothing? Aren't rocks supposed to have a life of their own?"

Granito tried pacifying Rocky, "Hey, we're rocks, after all, and that's how rocks are supposed to live, aren't they? What else can we do?"

This set Rocky thinking. "I shall avenge this mistreatment," it resolved. "I'll hit back those boys - hard. Yes! I must teach them a lesson." The idea thrilled it.

The next day, Rocky waited for the boys. When they came, a little boy kicked Rocky so hard that it flew high above the ground. It was the first time Rocky had been kicked so high, and it could see the entire valley from above. For a moment Rocky enjoyed the view. But revenge quickly eclipsed its sense of wonder. "I'll hit that boy's head," it thought, with anger driving its descent. Just as it was about to reach him, the boy ran away. Obeying the relentless pull of gravity, Rocky crashed to the earth with a jarring thud. It hurt as never before, and the pain added to its bitterness. Although the boys were just playing, with no particular malice toward Rocky, it became convinced that they came to the field solely to torment it.

Rocky constantly thought about being kicked, and the boys seemed to choose it above all other rocks. This made Rocky feel like a victim, thinking that the boys had something against it. Rocky didn't realize its own thoughts were attracting the kicks. The more it allowed these negative thoughts into its mind, the more the boys were drawn to kick it. It was all in Rocky's mind, yet it was completely unaware of the connection.

Day after day, the same scene repeated: Rocky was kicked high, briefly enjoying the view, but revenge and anger always brought it crashing back to earth, more miserable than ever. One day, brooding over its misfortunes, Rocky decided to escape to a far-off place, never to return to this land of kicking, hitting, and falling. It had no destination in mind, only a fierce determination to escape. "Falling somewhere else would be no different," it reasoned, "just different people who'd hit me again." "Today," it vowed, "I won't fall. I don't care about gravity. I'm going to defy it. I'm going to the sky!"

Evening came by, and so did the boys. The little boy who kicked hardest sent Rocky soaring. "No looking down," it told itself, "only up!" It maintained its airborne posture, channelling its anger and desire for revenge into upward momentum.

Up and up it soared, until it heard a voice call out, "Welcome, Rocky!" The Sky greeted it. Astounded by its own achievement, Rocky was speechless and could only stammer, "…Ummm…am I really here?"

"Yes, you are," the Sky replied with a warm smile.

 Rocky felt intensely hot. "Mr Sky," it croaked in a parched voice, "is there a river nearby? I'm thirsty!"

"What are you talking about, Rocky? There are no rivers up here. You feel hot because you're a star now. You sped so fast your whole being is burning. You're emitting light! Want to see your old home? Look at those boys who kicked you around."

Rocky looked down. It saw the boys gazing up in awe at its brilliant light. A surge of pride filled it. The boys who had once kicked and hit it now looked up to it with amazement.

It was a wonderful feeling—a feeling of triumph. Then the Sky asked, "Don't you want to thank those little rascals?"

"Why?" Rocky asked, confused.

"They're the reason you have been able to come this far, defying gravity, shining millions of miles away from where you started. They're the ones who made you rise above the dirt and mud you used to be in. They've brought about quite a transformation in you!"

Rocky was stunned to hear this. This was a totally new perspective that had never crossed its mind. It silently nodded struggling to accept the truth it had been blind to because of its negativity.

As Rocky became accustomed to its new surroundings, it learned that a star's life was far more complex than it had ever imagined. It wasn't easy. Rocky saw other stars shining brightly in the dark cosmos. They were beautiful and awe inspiring. They had provided light to countless planets for eons. But their existence was a constant struggle between balancing the pull of gravity on their mass and the energy loss through emission of light. A star's survival depended on perfect equilibrium between these opposing forces. Giving into gravity meant collapsing into a black hole, and emitting too much energy could mean a catastrophic supernova. Death lurked on either side of their existence. Yet, these stars believed their struggle was worthwhile, given the light and life they sustained across the universe.

They inspired young stars and served as role models. Just as DNA encodes all the information needed for a living organism's development, function, and reproduction, a star's energy wavelength patterns provided the blueprint for development of new stars. Rocky realized that inspiration, like energy, is essential for growth and survival.

Rocky still had much to learn. Life as a star was proving even harder than being a rock. No one kicked it, stepped on it, or sat on it anymore, but this existence had its own challenges. No one could approach it; it was too hot. It was intensely lonely. It even missed Granito. Up here, stars had to maintain their distance to avoid catastrophic explosions. Rocky couldn't accumulate too much mass; as the increased gravity would eventually lead to its demise. Any mass it did gather had to be burned to maintain equilibrium. Yet, it couldn't overexert itself, or finish two days' work in one, as excessive energy output meant a supernova. Star life demanded rigorous discipline, a precise balance of input and output.

Rocky gradually adapted to its star life, but it often longed for its days as a rock, sighing, "Those were the days!"

Discontent remained its constant companion. Yet, as it reflected, Rocky realized it didn't want to return. It didn't want to be kicked around by the riverbank again, nor did it truly enjoy its existence as a star. What was it to do then? It failed to understand why it couldn't find happiness either as a rock or a star, while other rocks and stars seemed to live a fairly normal and happy life.

Looking down, Rocky saw Granito, who was now shaped into a beautiful sculpture, admired by the other rocks. Granito had been happy before; now it was even happier. The other rocks looked on in awe, hoping for their own transformation. Rocky felt a pang of regret. "If only I had stayed…" it thought. Just then it noticed something inscribed on the statue's base. It read: "Contentment is the key to happiness."

The words struck Rocky deeply, and it understood: "Discontentment can never bring happiness, even if you reach the sky. But contentment brings joy, even while you sit in the dust."

Nobody Wins

"You can at the most be equal to someone, but you can never be anyone other than your own self!"

Varun and Rohit had been neighbours for years, but instead of friendship, their closeness had bred a rivalry so fierce that they measured their lives not by happiness, but by how much they outdid each other.

The two neighbours though living close to each other had pulled up a wall of competition between their existences to such a level that neither of them could bear to see the other. Yet they would peek over each other's house to get the latest news about what was going on and argue on unnecessary trifles whenever they felt the need to talk.

If Varun bought a new pair of shoes, Rohit would rush to the market to get the exact same pair—if not, a pricier one. When Rohit brought home a sleek white car, Varun followed suit with the same model, the same color. They copied each other crazily as if their lives were meant to be reflections of each other.

The things they bought or did were no longer about fulfilling needs or finding purpose and joy. It was all about keeping score.

One afternoon, they entered into a heated argument over the wall between their houses; with each one claiming to own it. Their tempers flared, and words turned to challenges.

"Enough talk!" Varun declared. "Let's settle this once and for all."

Rohit crossed his arms. "Name the challenge."

Varun glanced towards the swimming pool beyond their houses. "We jump into that pool. Whoever jumps farther, wins."

Rohit smirked. "Fine. And to make it fair, let's have Ramu Kaka, to be our judge."

Ramu Kaka, the community sweeper, was an old man. He had watched their childish squabbles for years. When Rohit and Varun requested him to judge their challenge, he sighed at their silly idea, but agreed.

Standing near the poolside the neighbours got ready to take the plunge. Varun took a deep breath and leaped. Rohit followed a moment later. Water splashed in every direction.

Varun surfaced first. "Ha! I jumped five inches farther than you!" he shouted, waving triumphantly.

Rohit turned to Ramu Kaka. "Tell him he's wrong! Who really won?"

The old man looked at them, the two grown men, dripping wet, their pride tangled in a meaningless contest. He shook his head.

"You both lost."

Varun frowned. "What do you mean? I jumped farther!"

Ramu Kaka sighed. "Five inches ahead or five inches behind—what difference does it make? Is the outcome of falling ahead or behind any different? Both of you fell into the water and are standing here, soaked to the bone. Did any of you gain anything?"

All of them were silent.

For the first time, Varun and Rohit were left speechless. They stared at each other, their rivalry suddenly feeling hollow.

Without another word, Ramu Kaka picked up his broom and walked away, leaving them to reflect on the foolishness of a race that never had a real finish line.

A Matter of Time

It was a quiet Saturday afternoon. Sheila stood by the closet, sorting through the clothes, setting aside those that had shrunk to be donated and those too worn to wear, to be used as dusters. She took pride in repurposing and reusing things, as it felt both environmentally friendly and economical. Besides, repurposing ignited her creativity.

One of her son's vests had a hole, so she added it to the pile of dusters. After a few uses, the vest that was once spotlessly white, turned grey and stained with dirt and grime. Even after a wash, the stains refused to leave the fabric, but she didn't mind. After all, it was only a duster.

One day, Sheila washed this old vest alongside other clothes, including her son's new vests. As she hung them out to dry on the line, her son joined her. The fresh vests were bright and clean, while the old vest, now a duster, was still grey and stained. She pointed the two items to her son, smiling wryly, "Look at the difference," she said, trying to highlight the difference in the appearance of the new and old vests.

But her son, seeing it differently, replied, "What is the difference Ma, that one was a vest few days ago, and this one will become a duster after some days. It is only a matter of time."

The profoundness of his simple words struck her and she paused, pondering as she allowed them to sink in. The little child had unknowingly highlighted a stark reality of life -   how time leads to change in appearance, which in turn changes the value, purpose and role of things. She thought about her own life, about how time would alter her position and role in life. What would her value be when she grew older? Would she become like a duster that could be discarded anytime?

As if reading her thoughts, her son placed his arms around her and said, "Just like when you grow old, you'll cleanse us with your wisdom, and won't need much cleaning yourself."

His warmth and wisdom made her smile. She felt at peace realizing that time had a way of reshaping everything, and accepting the change with grace is wisdom. Indeed she would become like the duster; no longer needing to shine, but always offering her presence to make her children shine.

Differences Don't Create Conflict

Nandu was tending to the kitchen garden when his daughter Lila playfully skipped over and asked, "Baba, why are all the people in the world so different? Are these differences the reason they disagree and fight with each other? Would there be more peace if everyone was made the same? "

Nandu smiled and took little Lila in his lap. "Look at this garden. I sow different seeds here—some grow into tomatoes, others become cucumbers, and some take the shape of melons. But the soil, water and sunlight are the same for all."

 Lila listened intently as her father continued, "You see, here on this farm, the same soil takes up so many different forms depending on the seeds sown. Some, like mangoes, turn sweet and hang up in the air from trees, while watermelons absorb too much water, growing sweet yet heavy, so they sit on the ground.

The tomatoes are not so ambitious and grow as small, tangy shrubs, while lemons, sour by nature, guard their sharpness with thorny bushes. Oranges mix sweetness and sourness, and the spineless bitter gourd crawls along the earth. The Neem tree, though bitter, stands tall as a healer, just like the humble basil! The mint and coriander, though small and soft, have an aroma that makes them the topping of most foods.

Corn, wheat, and rice yield many nutritious grains and hide them in their sheaths to protect them from pests. Some, like potatoes, carrots, and turnips, are shy and grow beneath the soil, while others, like this chilli, are small but have a fiery temper! Look at the cactus—it hoards water and bears thorns to protect it."

"But Baba, how come different seeds produce different manifestations of the same soil?" Lila inquired curiously.

"It's all about the recipe, dear — the thought or the idea behind the final product. Just as we can cook bread, *roti* or *poori* with the same wheat flour, oil and water, different seeds have different recipes to create different plants and fruits."

"Does that mean we can change ourselves into a totally different person by changing the thoughts or ideas in our mind?" Lila asked.

"You are right my child, by changing our thoughts and ideas, we can reshape who we become—just like a seed transforming into a unique plant.

This world is like a big farm where people adopt a form and behavior according to their innate nature and environment. But it is not the differences that create conflict. Differences bring variety and a range of possibilities. Conflict arises when we don't know how to deal with the variety available."

Lila looked at him thoughtfully, trying to absorb his words.

"Take this cactus, for example," Nandu continued, pointing to the prickly plant. "It may feel repulsive to have it in a farm, but

I can use it as a protective fence. When you know how and where to place individual characteristics in life, there is no conflict. You can then enjoy the variety."

Lila looked around at the plants, trying to understand how each one had its own place, its own purpose. Then, with a thoughtful expression, she said, "So, just like the plants, people are all different, but when we understand and respect their differences, there's no reason for conflict."

Nandu smiled warmly, feeling proud of his daughter's realization. "Exactly, Lila. The world is full of diverse people, each contributing something unique. It's only when we fail to understand and appreciate those differences that we create conflict. But once we learn how to place people in the right contexts, just like we do with plants, there's harmony."

Lila beamed, her face brighter with the wisdom she had gained.

Rendezvous with a Saint

The Sanskrit professor, Mr. Tripathy, had an unusual invitation for his students. "Would you like to meet a *sadhu*?" he asked one morning. The class stirred with murmurs and amused whispers —"A *sadhu*? In our town?"

Sadhu Baba was in town for a month, and Mr. Tripathy was arranging a meeting for students to meet him. Since he had taught them about the ancient language and its meditative roots, he saw this visit as an opportunity for them to learn about the spiritual lifestyle and gain deeper insight.

A few students laughed, while others exchanged curious glances. "Will he have long, matted hair and wear orange robes?" someone asked playfully.

Mr. Tripathy smiled. "Come and see for yourselves. He has agreed to meet those who are interested."

By the end of the discussion, several students, intrigued by the opportunity to meet a spiritual figure up close, decided to go.

The news became the topic of much discussion among the students. As they debated, their perceptions of a reclusive life surfaced. "Most people take up such a lifestyle because they have no other option," one said. "Maybe they couldn't find a job or didn't want to work hard for a living," another one added. Some joked that heartbreak might drive a person to seek solitude and the love of God. Laughter rippled through the group, their youthful minds tried to fathom why anyone would voluntarily choose such a life.

Dhruv sat silently, barely listening. His mind was elsewhere— wrapped around the pain of lost love. The girl he loved deeply had abandoned him, leaving him shattered and despondent. When his friends mentioned heartbreak as a reason for renouncing the world, his ears were drawn to their words. They seemed to have touched the raw wounds of his aching heart. "Can solitude or the love of God, mend a heart broken by love?" he thought.

Sadhu Baba was not very famous as he kept a low profile and had been living in seclusion for a long time. He stayed in an ashram adjacent to an old temple on the town's outskirts. Only a few people visited the temple occasionally, as it was quite far from the town center.

The students, accompanied by Mr. Tripathy, bicycled their way to the ashram. Some of them carried small offerings of flowers and fruits for Sadhu Baba and his disciples. They set off at 8 a.m.; it was a long journey and it took them almost an hour to reach their destination. The sun was already high, and the heat pressed upon them.

They were led to an open courtyard where floor mats were spread beneath the shade of a large tree. Sadhu Baba sat there in a lotus posture, welcoming them with a serene smile. They settled on the mats in a semi-circle before him, sitting quietly - absorbing the tranquility of the place. After a moment, Mr. Tripathy invited them to ask questions.

The first one came from Deepa, "Baba, why do we close our eyes for meditation? Can't we meditate with open eyes?"

The saint smiled. "Yes, one can meditate with open eyes, but it is an advanced practice. Closing the eyes helps clear the mind by reducing visual distractions. This also trains it to be more attentive by focusing on listening. Listening quietens the mind, because when it listens, it doesn't speak - its chatter silences. This improves receptivity and makes the mind open to receive the universal knowledge. That's why deeper truths are revealed during meditation."

Another student asked, "Is it necessary to renounce family life in order to meditate?"

Baba shook his head. "Not at all. Meditation doesn't discriminate between a householder and a monk; success in meditation is all about ones dedication to it. But just as closing your eyes helps to improve focus, solitude also helps. A family life lived with awareness is like meditating with open eyes—it is more challenging but just as meaningful."

Baba's warmth and wisdom created a congenial ambience and the students were gradually opening up – asking more candid questions.

Riya leaned forward. "How does meditation help in daily life? And how are you useful to the world sitting here in the forest, away from society?"

Baba chuckled then replied sagely, "We are accustomed to measuring worth of things and people by mere usefulness. But utility is only a small part of our existence which is a much greater reality.

Do you ever question the usefulness of a mother caring for an infant at home? The child is helpless and fragile - it needs nourishment, support and guidance before it steps into the world. The mind is like a small child. It needs to be nourished and strengthened before it is engaged in the world. If left uncared for, it is prone to mishaps, it can get run over by ordinary worldly things.

Unfulfilled desires, losses, snide remarks, competition, comparisons, failure, depression and setbacks can make a person suffer continually if the mind is not strengthened. Meditation is the training that makes the mind strong and 'suffering-proof' by nurturing and guiding it with inner light and awareness. Just like a child must first learn to walk at home before venturing onto the road, the mind benefits from meditating in solitude before entering worldly affairs."

The students nodded in understanding as Baba finished explaining. Just then, Mukul raised his hand, "Baba, how did you come to choose this path?"

Baba's eyes filled with old memories as he gazed into the distance. "My parents were a devout couple. Holy men often visited our home. I grew up listening to their wise words, from a very young age. My mother sincerely wished that I should dedicate my life to the service of God. All this greatly influenced my life decisions. While I was studying engineering,

I made up my mind that after completing my studies, I would fulfill my mother's wish and devote my life to divine love."

The students murmured, astonished at his mother's wish for such an austere path for her son. More than that, they struggled to understand how one could love an unknown and unseen entity.

Vyas voiced their thoughts. "How can we love God if we can't see Him?"

Baba smiled. "You do not see a tree in a seed, yet you plant it and nourish it with faith. Love for God is the same. You plant the seed of devotion in your heart, water it daily with His remembrance and it grows. It's that simple."

Dhruv, who had been silently listening so far, spoke for the first time. "No, it is not that simple. If the one you love breaks your heart, will you ever be able to love again?"

Baba smiled, and spoke in a compassionate voice, "Dear, love doesn't break hearts, it is meant to bring them together. Love is like water, it simply flows. It is our expectations that break. It is the absence of love that causes the cracks. When you seek love, you declare a lack of it within. Instead of seeking, grow love within yourself and share it freely without any expectation of return. Those who truly love do not ask for love in return; they have enough to give to the world."

Dhruv, still unconvinced, asked again, "But does one's heart need to break for the love in it to flow to the world? Many poets and saints yearned for God after heartbreak and ended up loving the world. Is pain necessary to release this love?"

Baba gestured toward the kitchen. "Fetch some tea from my disciple."

Confused but compliant, Dhruv returned with a tray of cups and a kettle. Baba took an empty cup and, to Dhruv's shock, smashed it onto the ground. "Now that it's broken, has any tea flowed from it?"

"Of course not," Dhruv exclaimed. "It was empty!"

Baba nodded, then picked up another cup and filled it to the brim. Slowly, he poured more tea, allowing it to overflow. "See? The full cup spills effortlessly. The heart doesn't need to break for love to flow—it only needs to be full enough to overflow. A broken heart with no love in it cannot pour anything into the world."

Dhruv stared at the saint, stunned by his simple wisdom. His mind absorbed the lesson as Baba's words resonated within him, sinking into the wounds of his heart like a soothing balm. A smile played upon his lips—a smile of realization and relief. He realized that it was expectation of return that had caused the pain, not love. In that moment he resolved to grow love in his heart. So much love as to fill it completely and pour it to the world without needing it to be returned.

Shortly afterwards, the students and Mr. Tripathy paid their respects to Baba and prepared to leave, but Dhruv remained seated, lost in deep thought. Something in him had shifted.

When his classmates called out to him, he simply waved. He was staying back. He had found his path.

Duty and Love

Sometimes, life brings us to some difficult crossroads, pushing us to make some difficult choices. At a time when what seems right in one dimension, doesn't seem so in another, the decision is hard to make. But then we all find the way.

Kay stood determined, guarding his line of control, as chaos reigned over the battlefield. Surrounded by smoke, gunfire and the cries of wounded soldiers, his eyes peered through the rifle scope. He took note of every movement on the other side of the borderline. Sparks flew through the enemy soldier's gun across him. As Kay focused, he resolved to bring him down. With grim determination and adrenaline coursing through his veins, he aimed at that soldier.

As he squeezed the trigger, hitting the soldier in front, throwing down his face guard, Kay felt a bit uneasy. The stumbling soldier looked strangely familiar. He bore a striking resemblance to a face from his past. As Kay recalled the familiar face, his heart filled with guilt and remorse. It was Bill - his childhood friend.

A cold dread settled over Kay. He had just fired upon his dearest friend. A conflict raged within him, a battle more fierce than the one he was facing on the field. Duty called him to continue the fight, to eliminate the enemy. But a deeper instinct urged him to rush to Bill's rescue, to offer aid, to defy the orders that had pitted friend against friend.

He knew if he would cross over to the other side to save him, he would be showered with bullets. But there was this strong impulse to save Bill. Kay knew that as a soldier it was not the right thing to do, but to stay back didn't seem the right thing to do as a friend. He reasoned with himself, "Who am I? A soldier? A friend? Or a human?"

In that moment memories of the time spent with Bill, flashed across Kay's mind. The days they went to school together, playing pranks, sharing everything from tiffin, laughter, secrets, and dreams of future. He remembered how they both had dreamt of joining the army in their own countries. At that time they hadn't imagined they would end up facing each other on the battlefield. He recalled the day he had enrolled for this ideal of patriotism. It all seemed to lay shattered and the war itself now appeared meaningless.

With a heavy heart and tears in his eyes he took the decision. He dropped his rifle and sprinted towards Bill, heedless of the bullets whizzing past him. As he reached his friend, he saw the life fading from Bill's eyes.

"Kay," Bill gasped. "If you've come to save a friend, go back, but if you've come to save a 'soldier from the other side', then save them all, Kay. Go call for a ceasefire."

Kay looked into Bill's eyes and said "I have come to see my friend, the one who fought with me as an enemy, and beyond these two, the one who is as human as I am."

"Go back Kay!" Bill cried with tears flowing down his eyes.

Kay hugged him one last time, before Bill finally lay dead upon the floor.

Kay's heart shattered .As he turned to return, he carried the weight of the world on his shoulders. The war, the patriotic spirit, the surge for conquest, everything seemed so meaningless in the face of the love that connects two humans.

In Bill's last moments as he held him in his arms, he realized that love knew no borders. "These imaginary lines on maps only serve to divide us. The role of a soldier that I once held in such high regard, now appears so small in the face of our brotherhood." Kay thought aloud.

The war, the bloodshed, the personal loss, led him to a profound realization, as he spoke to himself —*"Fulfilling your duty can take you to great heights, but love — it takes you beyond that."*

He felt a new sense of purpose rising within him and vowed to dedicate his life to fostering peace and understanding. He resolved to become a bridge between nations. He decided to live as a hope for humanity in a world torn apart by conflict.

In the years that followed, Kay became a renowned peace activist, traveling the world to spread his message of love and oneness. He spoke to leaders, inspired the masses and worked tirelessly to create a more harmonious world. And though Kay could never bring back Bill, through his work, restoring peace and love beyond borders, he always kept Bill alive in spirit.

Other Publications

<table>
<tr><td>Song of the Being</td><td>Untie Your Soul & Other Poems</td></tr>
<tr><td></td><td></td></tr>
<tr><td>Serene Illuminations</td><td>Perceptions</td></tr>
<tr><td></td><td></td></tr>
</table>

<table>
<tr>
<td>

Whispers from Eternity

</td>
<td>

Poby & Polly – Exploring Life

</td>
</tr>
<tr>
<td colspan="2">

</td>
</tr>
</table>